A Helluva Holiday

Jerrie Alexander

A Helluva Holiday

Jerrie Alexander

COPYRIGHT ©2013 by Jerrie Alexander

Published in the United States of America

Dedication

To my guardian angel, Alexa.

Chapter 1

Nate Wolfe hung up the phone, texted the rest of his team, and then went upstairs in search of his wife. Kay was standing in front of the fireplace. Their son, Kevin, watched from his playpen staring wide eyed as his mother put sparkly, bright colored objects on the mantel. Nate crossed to her, gently sliding his hands around her waist.

She leaned back against his chest. "Why do I think you have bad news?"

"Two more of our Lost and Found family members won't be here for the reunion."

"Jake and Holly Donovan aren't coming."

"Not this year; his aunt and her husband are joining them at the ranch."

"That's too bad." Kay turned in his arms. "I didn't expect Ty and Ana to fly all the way from Colombia but..." Kay left her sentence unfinished.

"They will be with us in spirit. The Christmas Day reunion will come off as planned."

****

Page Parsons didn't sneak anywhere and especially not into Eden Rock, Texas, with its population of 168,483. She was simply arriving late, not slinking in after darkness. Unless things had changed, the sidewalks had been rolled up and everyone was tucked in bed.

The two-and-a-half-hour drive west from San Antonio had put her in the heart of the little town right on time. Judging from the addition of a red light, increasing the number to three, Eden Rock had grown since Christmas five years ago, which was the last time she'd been home.

The friendly addition of red and green holiday decorations wrapped around the street lights welcomed passing strangers as they traveled through on their way to bigger, more affluent cities. A grin tugged at her lips when she discovered that two things had remained the same. The service station and the Dairy Dream were still the only businesses open at ten-fifteen at night.

The Dairy Dream windows displayed Christmas decals of a snowman eating a giant burger. Page's stomach growled at the thought of food. She'd been too busy packing and getting out of town to eat. Tomorrow she had the interview of a lifetime, and good nutrition had taken a back seat to creature comforts such as regular meals.

She lifted her foot off the gas pedal and coasted slowly past her old hangout. The young girl behind the counter couldn't have been much older than sixteen. Page was at least ten years older, which made her confident they'd never met. She made a quick U-turn and pulled up to the drive-through window.

The girl slid back the glass and asked, "What can I get you?"

"I'll have a cheeseburger with lettuce and tomato. No onions and easy on the mayo."

"Something to drink?"

A long lost memory slipped into Page's brain. "I want a small chocolate-strawberry shake."

"A small chocolate and a small strawberry shake?"

"No. Mix the two ice creams together in one cup, please."

"Okay." The girl's eyebrows lifted as the window closed.

Page needed to get to the ranch and get a few hours sleep. She'd drive to Houston tomorrow and arrive in time to hit the hotel spa. She'd be pampered and poised for Monday morning's interview.

A woman ran out the Dairy Dream's side door waving her arms. The bottom dropped out of Page's stomach. She remembered June Waller as being the worst gossip in town.

"Carol Ann Penny? Is that really you?" June slid to a stop at the hood of Page's car. A wise grin spread across June's face. "The minute I heard that drink order, I knew it was you. Get out of that car and come give me a hug."

Page abandoned the name she'd picked for her career and slipped on Carol Ann Penny. It felt like a warm sweater in the middle of winter. She eased out into the narrow space between her car and the exterior of the building, walked to her old friend, and opened her arms. "June, what are you doing here this time of night?"

"I'm the night manager. I got a promotion six months ago." June held Carol back and looked her over. "Woman, you look great. It's *you* I want to hear about. Come inside."

"It's late. You must be about to close."

"Nonsense. Park around front and come inside," June insisted.

Carol surrendered and did as instructed while June waited. She caught Carol by the hand, pulled her inside and into a booth. There was no doubt about what was about to happen. June was going to want to know everything that had happened in the five years Carol had been gone. She wasn't used to being on the opposite side in a Q & A session, but she'd also learned how to avoid answering questions.

"Manager? Congratulations." Carol tried an end run to avoid being quizzed.

"That's nothing compared to you. Our very own Carol Ann Penny on KWTA television. Everybody in town watches." June paused. "I'm sure Clay Hudson watches."

"I hadn't heard he'd moved home." Carol bit back the urge to ask more about the guy who she'd never been able to replace in her heart. "He's probably married with four boys by now. If he watches, it's for the news."

"He's been back a few months. Set up his veterinarian practice right next to the feed store. I heard he never married. Lord knows it couldn't have been for the lack of women trying."

Carol's heart fluttered at the thought of seeing Clay again. He'd gone off to college and then joined the Navy. No doubt, he'd come home a decorated hero. She, on the other hand, had attended college and worked her way to anchor the six o'clock news. Now she was coming home with her tail tucked between her legs. Neither Clay Hudson nor anyone else in town needed to know she'd been fired.

The young girl brought Carol's dinner out on a red plastic tray. The aroma of the greasy burger sent her appetite into overdrive. She removed the paper wrapper and took a bite, closing her eyes to wallow in pure unadulterated flavor.

"Still the best burger around?" The pride in June's voice rang true.

"Yes. I think my taste buds cried." Carol washed down the bite with a sip of the most amazing shake ever. "I'm glad I stopped."

"Does this mean the sale of the ranch is about to be final?"

"Looks like it." Carol wasn't surprised at June's question. The ranch had been on the market for a long time. "Sue Ellen and I both have to sign the contract."

"What's she going to do with herself?"

"She's taken a teaching position in Waco."

"I hadn't heard that. It's probably best for her. Losing Dan was a tragedy for sure."

"She tried, but after the accident, I think it became too much. The company that's buying the place has agreed to keep the place going." June's expression changed as her eyebrows drew together. Carol waited for a comment. When June remained quiet, she finished her meal and polished off the shake. After a short but awkward silence, Carol said, "I'd better get moving. She'll be worried about me if I'm not there soon." She dug out money to pay for the burger.

"Your money's no good here. That was on the house." June walked Carol to the car. "You stay in touch."

"Thanks for dinner."

Carol drove away wondering why Clay had never married. Minutes later, she checked her rearview mirror and watched the Christmas lights fade. The scene with her news director played through her memory. Things had gotten ugly after she'd delivered a story that she'd taken the word of a particular political figure to be true. Not to verify and check out her source was the kiss of death in journalism. It had been a stupid move and had cost her the job she loved. Her boss had fired her on the spot.

She shook off those memories when she realized she'd driven past her turn. A quick U-turn took her back to the cutoff. She drove down the familiar farm-to-market road that would take her to the Four-Penny Horse Ranch. Page Parsons ceased to exist out here. Carol Ann Penny would soon be home.

A boulder grew in her chest because, in reality, it was the Two-Penny Horse Ranch, soon to dissolve to zero. She had been six years old to Sue Ellen's eight when their father had died in an oil rig accident. How her mother had kept the ranch, even growing it into a prosperous business was a miracle. She and Sue Ellen had helped, but Carol would always believe her mother's heart attack was caused by overwork.

That the outside lights were bright enough to use as a runway didn't surprise her. It was the barn doors standing open, lights on, and a pickup parked in front of it that scared her. Something was wrong if her sister was out there this late at night. Carol parked and hurried inside.

"Sue Ellen?" Carol called out.

"We're back here."

She ran to the back stall where her sister and Clay were kneeling by the rear end of a mare about to give birth. Carol slid to a stop. Her jaw dropped and her heart pounded painfully against her ribs.

"Go around to her head and try to calm her down. Sit on her neck if you have to but keep her down," Clay barked instructions without lifting his head from the job at hand.

His voice snapped her out of her trance. The horse was in distress and needed help delivering the foal. Carol started talking softly to the mare as she moved up the side of the stall away from the horse's hooves. The past became the present as she dropped to her knees without thought. Their mother's years of raising quarter horses had been passed down to her daughters. Carol covered the mare's eyes with her hand and chanted soothing words. Minutes after she'd arrived, the foal was born.

"Wow." Sue Ellen pushed her hair off her face. "She had me worried for a while."

"It's a filly." Clay rolled the long plastic glove off his arm. His gaze lifted just long enough to catch Carol's and hold it for a second.

She almost had an out of body experience as she watched her heart leave her chest, float across the stall and drop into his hand. The day he'd driven away to college, they'd promised to stay in touch. Both kept their word for the first year, but with his school a thousand miles away from hers, the communication had finally dwindled to nothing. Nobody was at fault. They just grew apart.

Carol released the mare. Mama immediately stood, sought out the filly, and then started cleaning her new daughter. Two arms grabbed Carol and hugged her tightly. Together, she and Sue Ellen walked to the front of the stall and left Clay to finish his work.

"I was getting worried about you."

"Sorry, I stopped in town for a burger."

"Rosie was in distress so I had to call Clay." Pink flooded Sue Ellen's face as if she were apologizing.

"It was the right thing to do."

Carol struggled to keep her composure as she turned to greet the man who'd only gotten more handsome with age. If he looked this good at thirty-four, what would he be at forty? Unable to think of one witty thing to say, she blurted out, "How are you?"

"Good." He stared at her for a second. "Should I call you Page or Carol?"

"Carol works." For the second time tonight, she slid back into the small town girl she used to be. And again, it felt good.

He nodded and then went back to checking out the filly. Carol took this chance to get a good look at him. She watched his large hands work gently as he listened to the tiny horse's heart. The dark gray T-shirt he wore moved as his muscles flexed. With his forearm, he pushed back a lock of thick dark hair that had fallen onto his forehead, before leaning back with a sigh. He moved around to the mother, giving her a thorough going over. His tone was soft and comforting. Finally, he pushed his tall frame to his feet.

"They're both fine. The best thing we can do now is leave them alone. She's a seasoned mom; she knows what to do."

"I can have a pot of coffee ready in a flash." Without waiting for a response, Sue Ellen jogged to the house.

"That wasn't too obvious, was it?" Carol stood alone in the barn with a man who should feel like a stranger. But she'd never stopped loving him and all those old feelings came flooding back.

He laughed that same deep throaty sound she remembered. "I'm glad she gave us a minute." He turned on the water hose, lathered and rinsed his hands, drying them on the roll of paper towels on the shelf.

"You are?"

"Yeah. Aren't you?" In long strides, he crossed the short distance between them. "You're as beautiful as ever."

Carol felt the heat rolling off his body warming her skin. "So are you."

He chuckled at that one. "How long are you staying?"

"Don't tell Sue Ellen, but I have a job interview in Houston on Monday. I have to leave tomorrow when we finish up at the lawyer's office, but I plan to come back for our last Christmas at the ranch."

Did a flicker of disappointment cloud his sexy brown eyes? "I was hoping you planned to stay for a while. Sue Ellen has been depressed after she found out the company buying this property lied to her."

"What lie? She hasn't mentioned any problems to me."

"She probably didn't want to worry you. Look, forget I said anything. I spoke when I should have kept my mouth shut."

"No, not at all." Carol's heart rate spiked. "What did they lie about?"

"She should be the one to tell you. It was good to see you." Clay stuffed his stethoscope into a bag and snapped it shut.

"Wait." She panicked at the idea of never seeing him again. "Have coffee with us, please." He hesitated; his gaze shifted away from her for a second. He'd never been able to refuse her anything, but that had been a long time ago. Did that still hold true? "And please tell me about this lie."

"It's pretty simple. I don't know how Sue Ellen found out, but the new owner is going to sell the horses and turn the place into a feed lot. This area is a good location to fatten cattle, but she's really upset."

"No, they aren't." Images of pens full of cattle raced through Carol's mind. The land that her family had cleared and honed into prime pastures for horses would be destroyed. "Sue Ellen has been very specific. That company promised the ranch would be kept up and running."

He cocked his head, lifted an eyebrow, and remained silent.

"I get it," she said. "In the true sense of the word, it will still be functioning, just not as a horse ranch."

"Sorry, but it's true."

Carol nodded. "I should have read over every piece of paper Sue Ellen sent me better than I did. Believe me. I will tonight. I'd really like to know why this company lied."

"Maybe they thought she wouldn't sell under any other conditions. There are at least four other places for sale in this area and one is located right on the highway."

"Then they don't need this particular ranch." Carol's stomach rolled. She'd believed a lie recently and had lost her job because of it. "I don't like liars."

"Me either." Clay dragged his fingers through his thick dark hair.

"There has to be a way out of the sale."

"If you're serious, I have an old Navy buddy who might help. He can look into the company. Maybe figure out why they want this particular property bad enough to lie."

"During the holiday season? He would do that?"

"I can ask."

"Then let's do it. I'll deal with the lawyer."

"I'll call my friend first thing in the morning."

The words hadn't left Clay's mouth before it hit her. "Wait, I can't do that to Sue Ellen. She's accepted a teaching position and is expected in Waco right after the holidays."

"You can manage the ranch until you find the right buyer." Clay started walking to the house.

"What? Are you crazy?"

He looked over his shoulder. "Not even a little bit."

Carol followed Clay down the path past the feed and equipment barn to the main house. His walk was that of a man who knew his goal and purpose. She was grateful that he hadn't asked why she was interviewing for a new position.

Clay wiped his boots on the mat and then held open the back door for her. "Let Sue Ellen tell you herself."

Carol nodded and stepped into the kitchen/dining room. Instantly, she was surrounded by warmth. From the soft beige walls to the bright curtains to the oversized table that would seat eight. As if there had ever been eight in their tiny family. The original plan had been to have an even half-dozen kids in the Penny family, but that never happened.

The aroma of coffee and something baking wafted around the room like welcoming hugs. She swallowed back a tear, realizing just how much she'd missed this place.

"Blueberry muffins will be ready in ten minutes. You two get a cup of coffee, sit, and catch up." Sue Ellen looked so much like their mother that Carol again blinked away a tear.

Clay filled his cup and blew across the top of the hot liquid. "I'm going to make one last stop to check on Rosie and the filly before I head home. It's you two who need to catch up. I'll drop this cup off tomorrow."

Sue Ellen nodded as she bent down to check on her muffins. "Thanks for coming."

"You bet. Call if you have any problems."

"I'll walk you out." Wanting just a few more minutes near him, Carol followed him out on the porch.

He stopped on the bottom step and turned around. His gaze met hers at eye level. Carol felt the zing of heat ricochet through her body all the way to her toes. For a long second, they simply stood in the moonlight in silence.

"I am glad I got to see you." Her hands remained at her sides even though she wanted to reach out and touch his face.

"Are you?"

"You know I am."

"Then you should go back inside."

"What? Why?"

"Because I'm going to kiss you if you don't."

Was he joking? Did he feel the immediate pull as much as she did? "Really?"

He moved up a step. "Really."

"Drive safely." She turned and almost ran back inside. Clay laughed as she hurried away. The sound was challenging and charming and full of promises. She closed the door quickly.

"What's he laughing about?" Sue Ellen asked.

"I have no idea," Carol lied, hoping the heat in her face wasn't noticeable. She got the butter from the fridge, pulled two small plates from the cabinet, and joined her sister at the breakfast bar. "We do need to talk."

Sue Ellen's sigh was audible. "He told you. I was going to as soon as you arrived but then Rosie went into labor. I heard what the buyers planned to do to the property, so I confronted the attorney handling the sale. He was upset and demanded to know my source, but I refused. It really pissed me off that he seemed to know the truth all along."

"Then we'll stop them. Let's go over the contract."

Tears slid down her sister's face. Tall, with sun-streaked brown hair, she'd always been the pretty one in the family. Tonight, she looked tired and worn. She and her husband had put a lot of work into this ranch before he died. Losing him had been hard on Sue Ellen.

"I'm tired, Carol Ann. Without Dan, my heart is just not here anymore. I see him around every corner. As much as I hate what will happen to the ranch, I can't give up my new job to stay here until we find a new buyer."

Carol pulled her sister into her arms. "We'll do whatever you want. I really don't have a claim on this ranch. You and Dan finished the dream that Mom and Dad started."

"That's foolish," Sue Ellen insisted. "This is your home too."

"But—"

"No buts. This is my fault. I can't look at the pasture without envisioning what it will look like in a few months."

They were startled to hear a quick tap on the door; then Clay stepped back inside. "Sorry. I have a question."

"Come in." Carol pushed the plate of muffins toward an empty chair. "We're talking about how to stop the sale."

Clay joined them but passed on the food. "What real estate company is handling the sale? And what's the name of the buyer?"

"It's not a real estate deal. We're selling the ranch as a business. Our lawyer said they contacted him with an interest in buying the ranch business and all its assets, which entails the horses, land, trucks, four wheelers, horse trailers, and tractor, everything down to the posthole digger. I guess that's why I believed Vega Industries intended to keep their word."

The buyer's name sent chills up Carol's arms. How had she missed that? She glanced at Clay. His deep frown told her he'd picked up on the name too.

"Who handled the sale for you?" Clay said.

"Rick Henley. He's a new attorney in town."

"He approached you, right?" Clay asked.

"Yes. He said he'd heard that Carol and I wanted to sell the ranch to someone who would keep it going. The last thing we want is for the place to become neglected and the horses left to fend for themselves. Rick explained that since this was a business sale, the attorneys for each party would hammer out the deal and write up the contract. Rick would speak for me and then he'd negotiate with the Vega Industries attorney. All Carol and I had to do was accept or reject the offer."

"Vega Industries?" Clay's tone had gone harsh. "Carlos Vega?"

Sue Ellen's face paled. "You don't think? Oh, crap. Surely it's not *the* Carlos Vega who owns this company?"

"I don't know, but Carol has asked me to look into the company."

Carol could only nod. A heavy weight had settled on her shoulders. If she'd done her due diligence, she and Sue Ellen could have shut off negotiations before they started.

"I'll see you ladies tomorrow." He nodded his understanding when Carol didn't offer to walk him out.

"I didn't bring my copies with me."

"I'll get you mine." Sue Ellen left the room.

Guilt swamped Carol. She'd been selfish, caught up in her own life, and she'd left her sister spinning in the wind.

Sue Ellen returned with a large manila folder. "Here's my copy of all the communications, every email, and plus the formal offer." She was pale and exhausted. "I'm sick that I didn't connect the name."

"Don't do that. I'm the one who should have picked up on it. You get some rest. We'll catch up in the morning. I'm still wide awake from the drive, and I've got some reading to do." Carol hugged her sister, went to her bedroom, and opened the folder. Shame for not studying her copies more carefully put knots in Carol's stomach as she read and reread the documents.

****

Carol woke with a sore neck. The pages had dropped from her hand and were scattered across the bed. She placed everything back in the folder, went to the kitchen, and then put on a pot of coffee. The clock read four-thirty but there was no way she could go back to sleep. It was too early to call her attorney friend, so she got her suitcase out of the trunk of her car, and then showered.

Dressed in jeans, a sweatshirt and tennis shoes, she took a mug from the cabinet, filled it, and then went out to greet the morning. A chill rushed over her as she walked off the porch and into the wind. This winter was proving to be particularly harsh by Texas standards, dropping the temperature to numbers usually not seen in December, especially this far south.

Stars filled the cloudless sky but offered little illumination on her walk to the barn. Once inside, she decided against the flood lights, settling instead for a single row of overhead bulbs.

The quiet did nothing to unscramble the thoughts running through her mind. Days of her youth played through her brain as she walked and remembered the first time she'd witnessed the birth of a foal—in this very barn.

Her parents had held true to their word, waking her and Sue Ellen in the middle of the night to witness the miracle of nature. Excited beyond words, she and her sister had run to the barn still in their pajamas, holding on to their mother as the baby came. Their father gave them old towels and allowed them to help dry off the small colt.

Carol sat on a bale of hay. The possibility of a new future began to take shape in her mind. Had fate sent her home just for Christmas? Or had she come home for good? Could she do it? Did she even want to? She'd wanted to get out of Eden Rock and into the big city so badly, but had she ever been truly happy? Had she subconsciously wanted to be fired?

A strange peace filled her heart as she looked around the barn. Hadn't her father always said the Penny family's roots were planted firmly here, just outside of Eden Rock? Her bank account was in good shape; maybe she'd been sent home to buy Sue Ellen's half. So many questions flooded her mind, not the least of which was the impact of seeing Clay.

Carol stood, walked to the small office in the far corner, pushed open the door, and stepped inside. Its appearance had changed over time, evolving from her father's, then her brother-in-law's confusing stacks of paperwork, to reflect Sue Ellen's more feminine domain. Family pictures decorated the single shelf and a stack of romance novels sat on top of the file cabinet. She sat at the desk and thought about Carlos Vega. He was beyond horrible.

Whether it was the despicable Carlos Vega or an entirely different person really didn't matter. The sale would not be finalized.

Chapter 2

Clay's night had been a long one. After seeing Carol at the Four Penny Horse Ranch, he'd gone home, showered, tried to catch a few hours shuteye. He should have known that wasn't going to happen. The name Carlos Vega had set his mental alarm bells ringing. That and the way Carol's eyes flared when he threatened to kiss her had him staring at the ceiling for most of the night.

He threw on clean jeans, shirt, socks, and a pair of work boots, before heading to his small kitchen area to make a cup of coffee. He filled an oversized cup and then dug through his junk drawer until he found the exact business card he needed. He checked the clock to ensure he had time before his first appointment and then dialed the number.

"Lost and Found. How can we help you?"

A baby cried in the background. "Don't tell me Wolfe's Pack has a new member."

"Nate's walking the floor with his son as we speak. Are you a member that's he's kept secret?"

"No ma'am, but I've heard a lot about you all. If he can spare a minute, would you tell him Clay Hudson needs to speak with him?"

"Certainly. Please hold."

Clay wondered if Carol might be right. Christmas wasn't a good time to ask for help, especially since he had a child.

"Clay," Nate's voice boomed through the line. "How the hell are you?"

"Great. I'm finally getting my clinic off the ground. Congratulations on the baby."

"Thanks. We're pretty proud of him. Kevin was born in the safe room right here at the compound."

"The word 'compound' makes me think you've done well."

"We've been fortunate. If you get tired of tending to animals, my offer still stands."

"I appreciate that, but I'm happy right here in Eden Rock."

"It's probably grown since I was there with you on leave."

"We're closing in on two-hundred-thousand population."

Nate chuckled. "So, is this a social call or do you have a problem?"

"I have a friend who could use some investigation work done."

"How serious is this?"

"Things are peaceful and I'd like to keep it that way," Clay explained the situation and that the Penny sisters had decided to not to sell the family ranch. "This company lied to these two women and their entire ranch is about to go away."

"This sounds like a job for a good attorney."

"I agree, but Carol Penny would like to know exactly who is behind the lies and false promises."

"Who is this woman who has your attention?"

"Actually it's Sue Ellen and Carol Ann Penny. They're sisters. I went to school with them."

"Wait a minute. That picture that hung in your locker, wasn't her name Carol?"

"You have the memory of a Missouri mule, and they never forget. And yes, that the same person."

"Okay. We're in. Give me the name of the company involved, and I'll start digging right away."

"Vega Industries." A knot formed in Clay's gut just saying the name.

"Fuck," Nate growled.

"Exactly. If my hunch is right, he's not going to take a refusal to sell lightly."

"We'll do some digging from here. If this company proves out to be a front for Carlos Vega, he's going to try to force the sale. I may head to Eden Rock. You got a place for me to stay?"

"I live over the clinic, but the couch is yours.

"Is your place large enough to accommodate my motor home?"

"The parking lot is plenty big. You think it will come to that?"

"I don't know, but I like to cover my bases. I need to be home before Christmas. My wife is planning a reunion for the team."

"I can't think of a better place to have a reunion than right here."

Nate laughed. "Tell that to my wife."

"I'm not sure I can best the woman who got you to walk down the aisle."

"I'll call you back."

"Good enough." Clay rattled off his cell number as he grabbed a power bar, which he ate while he walked down the stairs to his veterinary office.

He pushed open the door and went inside. As usual, Milly Simpson had already lined up his morning. Milly was semi-retired or so she claimed but was still one of the best vets around. Her age was a mystery to everyone in town, including Clay. Her hair was the color of snow, and the winter wind couldn't hold a light to the sharpness of her tongue. There was no doubt that he couldn't survive without her.

"It's about damn time. Mrs. Carthage is in examination room three with that cat of hers again, and she doesn't wait well."

"Who doesn't, Mrs. Carthage or the cat?"

Milly's head lifted and so did one of her eyebrows. "Neither. I took the creature's temp. It's normal, which is more than I can say for its owner."

"Don't you figure Mrs. Carthage is just lonely? That cat is all she has now."

"You're probably right." Milly's eyebrow relaxed as she handed him the file on Allie, which he opened to review. "Why didn't you finish the examination?"

"That cat remembers me sewing her up. She doesn't like me."

"Bull. Animals love you. You don't like Mrs. Carthage." He laughed.

"You got me. By the way, a little birdie told me that Carol Ann Penny has come home. What are you going to do to keep her from leaving again?"

"Nothing." Clay grabbed his stethoscope and head down the hall.

"Nothing?" Milly's words faded as he walked away. It was probably just as well if he couldn't understand her.

He knocked and opened the door to take a look at Allie, the cat. "Good morning. What's going on with Allie?"

"She's not eating."

Clay took the cat out of her arms and put her on the table. He checked her heartbeat and pulse for strength and quality. Then he gently palpated the stomach. "Is Allie an outdoor cat?"

"She goes and comes as she pleases."

"And you never had her spayed?" Clay couldn't help but think he had good news for Mrs. Carthage.

"She's pregnant?" Mrs. Carthage stood, picked up her cat, and held her in front of her face. "Babies? We're going to have babies?"

"Yes, ma'am. Felt like at least four in there." He finished his checkup and sent a much happier Mrs. Carthage and her cat on their way.

The rest of the morning flew by as he treated one after another animal, each with a family that counted on his help. Milly finally closed the door at noon. She'd open again at one o'clock and manage the office while he made his house calls.

"I brought a large bowl of homemade stew. Want some lunch before you head out?"

"No thanks." Clay slipped off the white coat he'd put on earlier and hung it up. She opened her mouth so he paused.

"Are you stopping by the Four Penny to check on the filly and mare?"

"I am."

"Was Carol Ann there before you left last night?"

"Yes, ma'am. And how did you know she was in town?"

As was her daily habit, Milly reached up to a rack shaped like a horseshoe and pulled down one of the dozen ball caps hanging there. She handed it to him. "June Waller spent half of last night calling people. Everybody on the south side knows it."

"Call me if an emergency comes up."

"I will if it's a large animal."

Clay made his afternoon rounds, answering the same questions again and again from his patients' curious owners. Was Carol Ann Penny really back in town? He responded with the fewest words possible, leaving out the fact her long blonde hair still hung to her shoulders and framed her beautiful blue eyes perfectly.

The drive out to the Four Penny Ranch came last in his long day. Clay drove down the dirt drive and parked next to an expensive sedan. It wasn't from around here or June would have known about that too. He stepped onto the front porch, hung up a strip of Christmas lights that had come unhooked and then knocked.

Sue Ellen opened the door. "Come in. Carol's friend the lawyer is here. He drove down from San Antonio to help."

That Carol had already called someone in to help pleased Clay. He followed Sue Ellen through the living room, past boxes of holiday decorations and into the kitchen. Sitting at the table, pouring over documents, a man was making notes.

"Clay." Her eyes sparkled. "Come meet Evan Place."

"Pleased to meet you." Clay shook the older gentleman's hand.

"And you." Evan removed a pair of wire-rimmed glasses and slipped them into his pocket. "I don't see any issues with refusing to sell. It's a business deal that fell through. Sue agreed to a letter of intent via email, but neither of you have signed the actual contract."

"It's that simple?" Sue Ellen asked.

"Yes. I'll see this through. Vega Industries might rattle a few bones and make noises about suing, but in reality, the decision to sell rests with you two."

Carol smiled, her face lighting up. "I'm so glad I called you; I can't thank you enough."

"Just wait until you see my bill." He laughed and stood. "I'll call you after I stop in town and let Mr. Henley know your decision is final, and that I am your attorney as of today. If he contacts you, remind him that he's fired and to direct any further correspondence concerning you two or the ranch to me."

"Clay is going to help us look into Vega Industries. Did you reach your friend?"

"Yep." A chill rushed through Clay's veins. "He's agreed to do some research for us. I'm going to check on Rosie and the filly." He shook Evan's hand. "Nice to have met you."

"My pleasure."

Clay stepped onto the porch and then called Nate, sharing the information Evan Place had shared. The sale was officially off.

He crossed the yard and started down the path to the horse barn. Questions swirled inside his head as he walked. Was Carol staying? Or had Sue Ellen given up on her idea of moving to the city? He paused and took a minute to scan the ranch.

Just a few years back, when Sue Ellen and her husband Dan decided to start a family, they remodeled the house. They had applied a faux brick front, which gave the large homestead a more modern appearance, while the wraparound porch kept a homey feel.

Over a hundred acres of land had been cultivated over the years into a nutritious pasture for horses. Two barns and a corral made the spread complete. But Dan was killed in a car wreck, leaving Sue Ellen without the children they both wanted. The thought that he should buy the ranch flitted through Clay's head and was quickly pushed aside. Although, Sue Ellen employed two local men who'd retired and wanted part-time work. Maybe with their help...no. He shoved the idea to the back of his brain. He entered the barn to the sound of a horse nickering, the deep-throated noise they made when communicating.

"Is that you, Rosie?"

He was rewarded with a louder sound. He grabbed a handful of hay and walked to her stall. She and her filly were standing as if waiting for someone to come. He let her eat out of his hand, before removing the halter hanging next to her stall and slipping it on her head.

"You ready to stretch your legs?"

"Hang on and I'll open the corral gate." Carol hurried through the barn.

"Thanks." He led the mare out of the stall, leaving the filly behind. Within a few feet, Rosie made a low grumble and the little horse followed them. "You were smart to call a lawyer you trust."

"I met him when I did a story on an apartment owner who refused to have the air-conditioning fixed. Evan made sure it happened."

When Carol swung the gate open, Clay released the horses, carefully securing the latch and climbed up on the top rail. He extended his hand but she was already climbing. "This is a good way to make sure the filly has her legs under her."

He tried to ignore her thigh touching his while they sat and watched the young horse learn how to run and explore her surroundings. Carol touched his arm.

"Are you glad you came home?"

"Absolutely."

"But you've been in foreign countries and big cities; isn't Eden Rock a little old fashioned for you?"

"Not at all. This place brings me peace. Besides the town has grown a lot since you and I were kids." He steeled himself, knowing he had to ask if she was staying. "How have you and Sue Ellen decided to handle things?"

"I'm staying. At least until the right buyer comes along."

"What changed your mind?"

"I don't know. I walked down to the barn early this morning and sat on a bale of hay. I stayed there for a long time, thinking about my situation and what I should do." She paused, closing her eyes for a second. "I was fired from my job, Clay. I rushed through my research on a story and didn't verify my facts. I was lied to and I knew better than to take somebody's word."

"That's why you want Vega Industries verified even though you aren't selling to them?"

"Yes. It was inexcusable that I didn't check them out in the beginning. Why I would do something so careless?"

"You're being a little hard on yourself."

"It got me to thinking. Why is all this happening? Is it to help me realize that I belong here?"

"That's a lot of thinking in just a few hours. Careful you don't let your emotions take over."

"I've canceled today's interview."

"So you're home for good?" This could be too much too soon.

"I don't know, but Sue Ellen deserves to move on with her life."

"And how about you? Don't you deserve to start over again, too?"

"That's a loaded question. One I'm not prepared to answer."

Chapter 3

Nate Wolfe spent the afternoon on his computer researching Vega Industries. He'd known the answers before he started, but it paid to verify. He'd been seconds away from putting together a plan of action when his wife came into his office. He was currently working at keeping an interested look on his face.

"I'm sure Kevin will appreciate Santa leaving him a pair of denim jumpers." He smiled as his son did his best to wiggle out of his mother's lap. "He's dying to get his hands on one of the hundred Christmas decorations you put out."

"He has to learn what he can and can't do."

"He sure doesn't like being told no. I'm thinking he got that temper from you."

"That's one black mark for you on Santa's list." She laughed at her own joke. "So maybe I over did the decorations a little." Kay sat on the couch across from his desk. "You haven't heard a word I said since your Navy buddy called with the name of that company. You're interested. I recognize that look in your eyes."

She knew him inside and out. And he loved her for it. "It has been a while since I personally took a case. This one has my attention."

"What makes this one different?"

"I thought it would be a simple and easy case. Just what we need before the holidays." He chuckled.

"And now you're not so sure?"

"I think Clay was right. Vega Industries is owned by a series of dummy companies from Mexico to Colombia and Bolivia."

"Can Ty help?"

"It would be nice since he and Ana aren't coming stateside for Christmas, but we're not tracking the flow of drugs or money from Bolivia. Not yet. Carlos Vega wanted this particular piece of property and we need to figure out why."

"He's that famous drug lord who never crosses the border. Well, he never gets caught in the U.S."

"Right. Eden Rock is only a couple of hours from Coahuila, Mexico. Maybe he's creating a new shipping lane from Coahuila to San Antonio."

Kay has scooted to the edge of her chair. "Or Houston. It's a clear shot."

"True. My gut tells me that Carlos Vega won't be happy to learn the deal for the ranch fell through. I have to alert Clay and the owners of the Four Penny Ranch to expect pushback. Dalton and Tank can nose around with some of the local informants. Marcus can talk to the Feds and Dallas Narcotics and see if they have anything they're willing to share. Secrets are rarely kept in the drug trade. Somebody knows something."

"And you?"

"If things get tense, we might have to take Kevin on his first road trip."

"I'm not sure that's a good idea."

"I have to do this for Clay, and I don't want us to be separated this time of year. Besides, we have enough help to manage the business without us for a few days. What do you think?"

"I think I need to mull that 'few days' over. In the meantime, I'll let those three guys know you want them in your office."

"Just Tank and Dalton, and tell them I'll be in with Marcus."

Nate read through the background report he'd ran on Carlos Vega. Educated in the USA, he'd gone home, killed his uncle, and taken over a small cartel. That was twelve years ago. Since then, the drug lord had grown into a formidable figure in the illegal narcotics industry. He had long arms and kept what was his—his.

Nate stood and walked to the first office down the hall. A gold sign on the door read Marcus Ricci. Nate pushed and polished it with the cuff of his sleeve. "Got a minute?"

"A minute? Take all the time you want. I'm fucking bored out of my mind." Marcus quickly looked past Nate. "Kay's not right behind you, is she?"

"No." Nate laughed as he sat across from his old friend. They'd been through a lot together since starting the Lost and Found, Inc. agency. He'd watched Marcus grow from a tortured soul to a happily married man.

"What's up?" Dalton Murphy said, as he and Tank Jorgenson walked in and sat.

"I'm taking a quick case to help out Clay Hudson, an old navy buddy."

"Thank God," Dalton said. "What do you need from me?"

Nate outlined what he'd learned. "Dalton, you and Tank go talk to the Dallas police department." He filled the three men in on the situation. All of them knew the history behind Carlos Vega and his empire.

"Vega isn't a good enemy to have. If he wants this ranch and this guy backs out on the sale, it could get ugly." Tank, the newest field member, grabbed his neck and mimicked a man being choked.

"He doesn't own the property, but he's friends with the two sisters who were duped into thinking their horse ranch would remain in business."

"You're right to help them out," Dalton said. "But this close to Christmas, you married guys have wives to keep happy. Tank and I are single. We can run point on this one."

"Thanks anyway. I'm taking this one. Clay saved my life while we were on assignment. If he's worried about these two women, so am I. In fact, I've already offered to go to Eden Rock."

Marcus beamed across the desk. "It would be fun to have you back in the field, but have you cleared it with the boss?"

Tank elbowed Dalton and both rolled their eyes at Marcus's reference to Kay as the boss.

"Be wiseasses now. One of these days you'll both be in the same boat with me and Marcus. But to answer the question, she's thinking about coming along. I'll take the motor home so she and Kevin will be comfortable." Nate turned to Marcus. "You've made some contacts. Talk to as many as you can. Somebody knows why Vega wants this property."

Dalton leaned forward, placing his forearms on his knees. "I'll check with the FBI too. Vega is on the most wanted list so they are keeping tabs on him. Maybe they have some intel they will share, but if he decides to retaliate against the sisters, we could be celebrating the holiday in Eden Rock, Texas."

****

Clay's mind kept wandering to Carol. This morning he'd been in the middle of a juicy dream when the alarm clock jarred him into reality. He finished wrapping the dog's paw with gauze. He and Milly had treated the stray for mange, given it an IV of fluids, and an antibiotic shot. The small animal rescue group in town had found the poor creature living in an abandoned barn and brought him to the clinic for help. He carried him to a cage that would limit his movement, placed him on the old blanket inside, and stroked his head.

"You're safe now, old fella."

"I'm going to name him Dancer," Milly announced.

"He's an old man. There's not much dancing left in him."

"Where's your Christmas spirit? Any strays that are brought in here between now and the New Year will be named after one of Santa's reindeer. If nobody claims the poor thing, I'll give him somewhere to live out his life where he'll be safe and have a full belly."

Clay washed and dried his hands, walked to Milly, and then tipped her chin up with his finger. She was barely five-feet-four inches tall, yet she looked up at him as if daring him to challenge her decision. "How many dogs will that make you?"

"Don't know and don't care. Then you take him."

"Upstairs?" He shook his head. "He'd have trouble going up and down the stairs."

"True. Maybe it's time you had a real home."

His cell vibrated before he could think of a snappy comeback, so he pulled it from his pocket and answered. "Nate. Good to hear from you."

"I'm not a bearer of good news."

"Go ahead," Clay said while walking into his office. He closed the door and then sat.

"Dalton Murphy still has ties with the Feds. Rumor is that Vega is planning to increase his shipments into the U.S. Could be he planned to use the place as a halfway mark or storage facility. Smuggle large amounts of narcotics to the ranch and then disperse it to parts unknown from there. The route is an easy drive."

"So you think Vega will just pick one of the other ranches in the area?"

"He's not known for taking no for an answer. If he comes back with a new offer, a second refusal will piss him off."

"I figured as much."

"I have a couple of men talking to a couple of the Dallas narcotic boys, too. They'll keep listening for information. Stay in touch."

"Will do." Clay removed his coat and hung it on the rack. "I'm square for the day?"

"Sure are. You go on. I'll catch anything that comes in."

"Thanks, Milly." He put on the ball cap she chose, jumped in his pickup, and then drove out to the ranch.

He pulled down the long driveway just as Carol walked out of the barn. The sun glinted off her hair. The cold wind lifted the long strands and she quickly covered her head with a cap. Wearing a sweatshirt, jeans, and boots, she waved and walked to meet him.

"You're just in time."

"For?" He got out and followed her to the barn.

"I went to the grocery story this morning and happened to see a truck unloading Christmas trees for the Lions Club. I bought a fresh cut Virginia Pine."

"And you need help getting it inside?"

"Sure. But first, I need it in that stand." She pointed to a big box. "Unless it's too cold out here for you," she added with a teasing smirk. "We can always carry the tree inside and then get it secured."

"I'm fine in the cold. Where are your gloves?" He took his knife out, opened it, and then passed it to her.

"I had already borrowed enough of Sue Ellen's clothes. I hated to ask for more."

Carol opened the carton containing the stand while he pulled the tree off the pickup bed. He stood it up. "Smells fresh."

"The inside of the house is going to smell great. They worked in silence until the tree was secure and ready to go. He reached through the limbs, grasped the trunk, and then carried it to the front porch.

Sue Ellen held open the door and directed Clay to a corner with a piece of plastic spread out on the floor. Elvis singing stopped her in mid-step. "That's my cell. I'll be right back,"

Carol slid the piece of plastic out away from the wall. "We'll need room to string lights and decorate."

"We?"

"You have a problem with the word 'we'?" She opened a weathered cardboard box marked *Lights* in black marker on the side.

Sue Ellen came into the room and walked to Clay. She tapped a finger to her lips. "Yes, I'm here. I'm putting you on speaker so my sister can hear."

Clay put his cell on record and held it next to Sue Ellen's.

"Go ahead, Mr. Henley. We're listening," she said.

"That's fine. You both need to hear what I have to say."

"Mr. Henley, this is Carol Penny. My sister has already informed you that we are no longer in need of your services. If your call concerns this ranch, you should contact Evan Place, our new attorney."

"Ms. Penny, Vega Industries contacted me personally with a request that you consider a new bid." Henley continued as if Carol hadn't said a word. "Mr. Vega has invested large sums of money into equipment for his new endeavor. He's willing to up the price."

"The ranch is no longer on the market," Carol said.

"Mr. Vega has threatened a lawsuit to recoup his losses."

"He can sue all he wants. If Mr. Vega needs to hear that again have him contact our attorney. Do not attempt to speak for us." Carol's tone was firm.

"You're making a bad decision." His voice had turned from pleasant to cold.

"Goodbye, Mr. Henley." Carol nodded at her sister who ended the call.

Clay shut off the recording. "We should talk."

"I'll get back to folding clothes," Sue Ellen said.

"I came to speak with you both."

"Then come to the kitchen and have a seat."

Clay followed the ladies to the kitchen and again passed on a bite to eat. Once he had their attention, he repeated his conversation with Nate. "Just as we expected, Vega Industries traces back to Carlos Vega. You should be ready for him to push back."

"He's not just dangerous, he's evil!" Carol wrapped her arms around her waist. "Some of the stories that came across the news desk had to be severely edited in order to air them."

"Are you suggesting that he might kill us if we don't sell to him?" Sue Ellen's voice had gone up an octave with each word.

Both women looked at Clay. Fear filled their eyes as they waited for his answer. No way could he lie to them. "I don't know. That he offered more money tells me he's determined."

"I'll bet Rick Henley was working for that bastard Vega from the beginning." Carol had shifted to anger. "He should be disbarred."

"Nobody has made any threats or broken the law. So we just wait for their next move?" Sue Ellen asked. "What do we do?"

"Legally nothing." Clay got up and paced. "If you stand firm, there's a chance that Vega Industries will find a new property that fits their use, but I seriously doubt it."

Sue Ellen stood. "The wash won't fold itself."

Clay rose and turned to Carol. "She's scared."

"We should be. This is my fault. I should have immediately questioned the Vega name, but I just scanned everything she sent me. Let the lawyers handle this was my mantra."

"Don't be so hard on yourself. You know that old saying; the horse is out of the barn. Now we fix things."

They walked back to the Christmas tree, and she pulled a long string of tangled lights from a box. Holding them out for Clay to take one end, he saw tears fill her eyes.

"We have a mess on our hands," she said. Her voice was as soft as when she'd calmed the mare.

She wasn't referring to the lights, so he took them from her and placed them on the couch. He was about to take a chance that could go really well or very wrong. He opened his arms and waited.

"Clay," she whispered, walking straight to him. Her hands went around his waist, and she rested her head on his chest.

He closed his eyes and held her close. Tight. Pressed her against his body. Allowed his skin to feel her warmth. How could you fall in love so hard, that many years later it was still this true and strong? He'd had other women but never loved anyone else.

"Too long," he murmured into her hair. "It's been too long since I held you in my arms."

He had no idea how long they stood there, neither daring to move or interrupt the moment. When she slid her hands from his waist up to his arms, he stepped back.

"I won't let anything happen to you or Sue Ellen. You know that, right?"

"Yes. I do."

"Then grab one end of that string of lights and hang on while I unravel them."

The comfortable, easy movement of readying Christmas lights for the tree relaxed them both. It felt as if they'd never been apart. They talked about high school friends, his practice, and her work while they decorated. She had no idea if he'd ever helped decorate for any holiday with any woman, and she didn't care. That could wait for another day.

"I'd forgotten how content I am when I'm here. How much I love this place."

The need to kiss her traveled through his body. "I should go."

"Why? We still have to finish the tree."

"Because if I don't, I'm going to kiss you," he said for the second since she'd come home.

"Don't let me stop you."

Clay pulled her into his arms, lowered his head, and then covered her lips with his. This was a soft gentle hello. He lifted his head and did it again; only this time her lips parted giving him access to her mouth. She smelled like Christmas and tasted like heaven. He ended the kiss, leaving her with something to think about.

Chapter 4

Carlos Vega slammed his cell phone down on his desk. His lit cigar flew off the ashtray and landed on the carpet. Ashes scattered, settling across the high gloss shine of the mahogany surface.

"Fucking whores." He stood shoved his chair back and pointed to the mess. "Get that cleaned up," Carlos instructed.

"Si, jefe." The girl was in motion seconds after he spoke. He studied her for a minute. What was her name? Did he want to know? Not at all. Virgins were his favorite, and this one couldn't make that claim anymore. When she finished, Carlos nodded to Ramon, who grabbed the puta and dragged her from the room.

Carlos walked over and studied the topographic map spread across the conference-sized table. His blood pressure was rising faster than his expenses on this project.

Ramon returned, opening the door partway. "The asesino is here. Want him to come in?"

"In a minute."

"You want construction stopped?"

Carlos caught Ramon's gaze and held it, biting back the urge to shoot him for such a stupid question. "No. I want you to find out how these sisters learned that I didn't give a shit about operating their ranch. I am bleeding money and time. The project must be completed in order to honor commitments I have made."

"I will see to it this person dies."

"Do that." Carlos nodded. "Show the kid in."

A few minutes later, a baby-faced young man entered. Tall and thin, his dark eyes reminded Carlos of a dead man's. Enrique Ortega was new to the business, but he came with good credentials. He'd already earned the reputation that he enjoyed his work. Carlos wanted to see if the young man could be useful in other ways too. He motioned Enrique to join him.

"You have something for me?" The kid took silent steps across the floor.

"Ramon told you about my project?"

Enrique shrugged. "I heard you ran into a problem."

"You heard right. I spent a great deal of money searching for the right location, and this piece of property will open a lane for shipments that will move a lot of product faster and safer. I will put feeder pens right here and grain silos here." He stabbed a spot on the map with his finger. "It's important that trucks coming and going become a common sight." Carlos rolled up the map revealing a second one with more detail. "The sisters who own this property are refusing to be reasonable."

"You want me to kill them?" Enrique's shoulders lifted as if he was bored.

"No." Carlos was constantly amazed at how people did not think ahead. "If they are both dead, the property will stay tied up in the legal system for years. First, the sisters must be encouraged to sell, and one must live. Use your imagination."

"Accidents are a common thing around a ranch."

"Exactly."

The kid turned and left the room. Ramon walked back in, looking over his shoulder. "That is one cold-blooded motherfucker."

****

Carol grabbed a horse halter and lead rope, pulled the cap Sue Ellen had loaned her over her ears and began her search. She called Pete as she walked. The gelding was always first in line for his share of breakfast and when he hadn't turned up, she'd volunteered to go find him. She'd walked a few hundred feet when she spotted him lying on his side, his thick winter red coat standing out against the dry brown grass. Carol ran, shouting Pete's name into the biting wind. She fished out her phone and dialed Clay's clinic.

Milly's voice came on the line. "Hudson Veterinary Clinic."

"This is Carol Penny. Tell Clay I have a horse down. I'm trying to get him up and into the barn."

"He's a couple of miles from you. I'll have him there in a few minutes." The line went dead.

Pete made a soft chuffing sound as he rallied enough to stand. She didn't try to put the halter on him; instead, she slipped the rope around his neck. She had to get him inside out of the cold. He wobbled as if drunk, but responded to her gentle pull.

"It's okay. We'll go slowly."

Sue Ellen stood at the back of the barn, holding the door open.

Step by step, Carol led Pete toward shelter, allowing him to stop and gather himself when necessary. She walked next to him as if she could hold his weight if he went down. By the time they'd reached the barn, Sue Ellen had shuffled horses around, emptying the closest stall. Pete stumbled inside and immediately stuck his head in the water trough.

Clay's slid his truck to a stop and ran to them. "Talk to me," he said as he went into the stall with Pete.

"He can barely stand. And is drinking water like he's been in a race."

Clay checked Pete's temperature and heart and then moved the stethoscope to his stomach. He lifted Pete's upper lip. He pressed two fingers against Pete's gums. "His gums are off color. Have you changed his feed?"

"No. He eats the same thing all the horses do."

"Could be colic. If it's his liver that's a bigger problem. I'll tube him. Expedite flushing out anything in his stomach. I'll take a blood sample but in the meantime, I'll give him a shot of neostigmine to be on the safe side."

Clay went to his truck and brought his equipment inside. Two hours later, Pete seemed to have turned the corner. He was weak, but he'd stopped drinking water like he was dying of thirst. Clay had checked the feed barrels and the hay for anything that might have caused Pete's illness.

He handed Carol her coat. "Show me where you found Pete."

They walked into the chilling weather and he wrapped his arm around her shoulder. She guided him to the spot. "This is about right."

Clay released her and walked in a circle around the area, widening the loop while keeping his gaze on the ground. He reached down and picked up something.

"Tomatoes will make a horse sick and most horses won't eat them."

"Don't look at me like that. We know better than to feed potatoes and or tomatoes."

"There a lot of seeds, stems, and pieces scattered across the ground here. None of the other horses have displayed any symptoms?"

"No, but Pete pees on hay to keep the other horses from eating it. Then he goes back and eats it later. Maybe he peed on the tomatoes."

Clay shook his head. "That habit may have saved his life. It looks like somebody intentionally threw the tomatoes into the pasture. You should call the sheriff."

Again he snuggled her under his arm on the walk back to the barn. They stopped and checked on Pete, who was munching on hay. Carol reached in and stroked the horse's muzzle while she filled in Sue Ellen on what Clay found.

"Then this was deliberate." Sue Ellen pulled her cell out of her pocket.

"We agree. I'll call the sheriff."

"That's a good idea."

Sue Ellen spoke on the phone for a few minutes, hung up and said. "Blake's on his way. I promised him a cup of coffee would be waiting on him." She left the barn and returned to the house.

"I still have trouble thinking of Blake Carson as the sheriff," Clay said. "But he's doing a good job."

"Has he gotten fat and bald?" Carol pulled off her gloves.

"Neither, but he did get married."

She caught Clay's face in her hands. "You're cold."

"I won't be for long." His lips covered hers.

The kiss by the Christmas tree had been a long, get reacquainted kiss. This time his tongue swept inside her mouth, lighting a fire that burned all the way to the bottom of her feet. Her knees had almost folded under her when he stepped back.

"Thanks. I needed that," he said.

Confusion swirled in her mind. He'd always held a special place in her heart, but that had been a long time ago. "Can we go back in time? Is that what we're doing?"

"I hope to hell not. That had us going separate ways."

"Right." She squirmed under his scrutiny. "Let's go inside where it's warm."

Carol helped her sister carry cups and a plate of cookies to the living room while Clay put a log on the fire. She was proud of their decorations. The room looked like a Christmas card with its ceramic knick knacks, candles, and her grandmother's nativity scene on the mantle.

"The sheriff is going to think we're having a party instead of reporting a possible crime," Clay said.

Sirens blasted through the air as the sheriff's car roared down the driveway.

"That's a bit of a dramatic arrival, isn't it?" Carol asked. She opened the front door and the obvious smell of burning grass filled the room.

"Fire," the sheriff called out as he ran toward the barn. Smoke rolled through the sky in the high wind.

Carol ran to the storage barn and grabbed two water hoses that had been rolled up and put away for the winter. Clay disappeared into the barn, and by the time she lugged the hoses out in the drive, Blake and Sue Ellen were there to grab them.

"Fire department is on its way," Blake said as Sue Ellen showed him where a faucet was located.

Carol dragged the second hose inside the barn where Clay had turned on the one he'd used minutes ago and was wetting the back side of the building down.

The dry pasture grass was burning rapidly and with the wind out of the north, it was headed straight for the barn and house. Lucky for them the sheriff's timely arrival had given them the time to get the fire under control before the fire trucks arrived. Before they left, the firefighters had ensured there were no embers left alive.

At the end of the day, everything was quiet. Reports had been filed, the coffee pot emptied, and she, Sue Ellen, and Clay sat on the porch steps too tired or too numb to notice the bitter cold.

"This is the worse winter we've had in years. I hope it doesn't get worse." Sue Ellen groaned as she stood. "I'm going inside. Thank you for your help, Clay."

"My pleasure." Clay stood and stared at the sky. "You should go inside too. Are you up for a drive tomorrow morning?"

"Sure. Where are we going?"

"Dallas. I think you need to meet my friend, Nate Wolfe."

****

Enrique drove to his motel, satisfied that he'd gotten the message across. He didn't know if the horse had died and didn't care. The fire had been an afterthought, but effective. The wind had blown a piece of newspaper at his feet, so he'd lit it, and then watched as the dry grass gobbled up the flame. Tomorrow, Carlos could extend a new offer to buy the ranch. If that didn't work, he'd pick one sister and kill her. His brand new Savage 110 Police and Military Tactical Sniper rifle with a bull barrel and red field scope fired a .223 caliber bullet. It was waiting in the trunk, and he was itching to try it out.

****

Carol wasn't prepared for the Lost and Found compound. She'd envisioned a strip center with a small office and a couple of men at desks behind the darkened windows. Obviously, she'd been watching too many old movies. The main gate was all that was exposed to the public eye and a man wearing a dark green t-shirt and pants stopped them at the gate.

"Good thing I called ahead," Clay said with a chuckle. "Nate wasn't exaggerating when he said the business had done well." Clay rolled down his window. "Clay Hudson and Carol Penny to see Nate Wolfe."

"Yes, sir. May I see some identification?"

Clay fished out his wallet and handed the man his driver's license.

"Thank you." The man returned the ID. "Take the first fork to the right. It will take you to the office."

The office was an understatement. The two-story building was huge. Red brick with oversized glass windows sparkled under the winter sun. Two smaller structures sat to the side. A man was inside a large fenced area playing ball with a dog.

"Did you happen to ask how much your friend charged for his services?"

"No."

A tall, sandy-haired man stepped out the front door and walked to Clay's side of the pickup, ending the conversation about money. He got out and the two shook hands and hugged, pounding each other so hard Carol realized she never wanted to be hugged quite that much. She got out of the truck and waited, enjoying the show of emotion between the two men.

"Carol?"

A beautiful woman walked toward them. On her hip rode a curly-haired baby, whose hands were both waving hello. Carol left the two men talking and joined the woman.

"Carol Penny. Who is this handsome guy?"

"This is Kevin Wolfe and I'm Kay. Let's go inside. Those two will be out here talking smack for a while." The little boy gurgled and held his arms out.

"May I hold him?"

"If you're sure. He drools on everything."

Carol took Kevin from his mother and followed her inside. He curled his hand into her hair as they entered a large room. Ten cushioned chairs surrounded the oval conference table. A whiteboard and a television took up almost one entire wall. One short wall was covered in monitors, the screens were constantly moving, she assumed to different parts of the compound.

She pulled one chair away from the table, sat, and rocked Kevin in her arms. His tiny body relaxed and he yawned. Slowly his eyes closed. "He's beautiful."

"You're a miracle worker," Kay said. "He's teething and no one has been able to calm him down. Want me to put him to bed?"

"Oh no. He's fine right here." Carol smoothed her hand over his forehead. "Tell me about this Wolfe's Pack."

"There's not a lot to tell. Nate started the company with the help of a couple of old college buddies. Marcus Ricci and Tyrell Castillo are partners now. Ty lives in Bolivia with his wife and handles cases from there. We've added Dalton Murphy and Tank Jorgenson plus seven fairly new members. One of Wolfe's Pack, as I dubbed them back during our college days, runs a ranch a couple of hours from here, but he's still part of the family. A lot of our work is for the government but Nate has held fast to his reason for forming Lost and Found, Inc. We help people with problems. Whether it's finding a missing person or protecting somebody from harm, we're there." Kay's cheeks flushed. "I'm sorry. That sounded like a public service announcement. The truth is we're a family. Blood or not, we're a unit."

"I like the way he thinks. I'm glad you told me." Carol didn't know how much Kay knew about the problem at the ranch, so she began at the beginning and brought her up to date. "Clay hasn't said much about Nate except they were in the Navy together."

"It must be some kind of code. They talk to each other, but they don't discuss their missions with anyone else. Here's one of the partners, Marcus Ricci."

The big man nodded as he walked down the hall. A beautiful black and brown dog with a shock of white around his neck trotted just behind him.

"Hello, I'm Marcus Ricci," he said stopping across from Carol. "You would be Carol Penny?"

She nodded admiring both the man and his animal, as both were quite attractive. "That's correct. Your dog is beautiful."

"Thanks. I thought I'd come in first and introduce you to Diablo."

Carol chuckled. "Diablo?"

The dog's ears turned and pointed at her.

"Hold out your hand palm down."

She did as instructed.

"Go ahead." Marcus pointed at her hand and the dog walked to her. He sniffed and then licked her hand. "You can pet him."

She leaned down, buried her hands in the thick fur around his neck, and scratched. "Aren't you a sweetheart?"

Chapter 5

Clay followed Nate inside, where he introduced his wife Kay. A man stood and extended his hand. Clay liked the firm handshake from Marcus Ricci. A dog sat next to the man's right foot.

"That a good looking animal." Clay held the back of his hand down so the dog could smell him.

"Thanks. He's a great companion."

Nate bent down and ruffled the dog's fur. "Can you believe he's a trained killer?"

"Not anymore. Those days a long gone from his memory," Marcus corrected Nate. "Although, we don't speak Spanish around him."

Kay stood. "Carol and I are going to put Kevin to bed. We'll be right back."

Cradling the infant in her arms, Carol followed Kay into the hall and up the stairs. A strange wave of heat slammed into Clay. The serene look on her face and the baby painted a picture in his mind he'd carry forever.

"We live upstairs," Nate said.

"I live over my business, but I'm guessing my efficiency is slightly smaller than your living quarters."

Nate took out his phone and tapped a message. "Dalton and Tank are at the firing range. They're joining us."

In less than five minutes, two more of Nate's team joined them; leaving Clay to believe the range had to be on the property. Nate introduced Dalton Murphy and Tank Jorgenson.

"Is it this cold in your part of Texas?" Dalton asked, pulling off a jacket.

"This winter has been the worst I can remember. We're further south than you guys, but Mother Nature hasn't spared us this year."

"As long as it doesn't snow, I'm okay with winter," Carol said. She walked around the table and sat next to Clay.

"Who wants to start?" Nate asked.

Clay slid his hand under the table and clasped Carol's hand. "Why don't you tell them about yesterday?"

The linebacker-sized man called Tank stood and leaned against the wall, as Carol recounted Pete's condition and the walk back to the barn. His jaw muscle noticeably twitched as she talked.

"To do that to a helpless animal takes the lowest scum of mankind," Tank said.

Nate smiled at the man's outburst. "Tank's family raises horses too."

"You're right," Carol agreed. "Somebody either knows about horses or did some research to learn that nightshade plants can be poisonous to them. We're lucky I found Pete in time."

"Did you report it?" Tank had pulled out a chair, turned it around, and straddled it.

"Of course. By the time the sheriff arrived, my pasture was on fire."

"How much was damaged?" Nate asked.

"Just dry grass, but the fire chief doesn't think he'll be able to determine the cause."

"Any lightning strikes around that time?" Marcus asked.

"None."

Nate raked his fingers through his hair. "Is everyone thinking what I'm thinking?"

"Road trip," Dalton said. "We'll need the name of a motel."

"Clay offered me his parking lot as a temporary spot for the motor home." Nate glanced at his wife. "Kay and the baby are coming with me."

"Then you, Kay, and Kevin will stay at the ranch." Carol held up her hand. "Don't argue. There are two extra bedrooms and a second bathroom that only have the doors opened when someone goes into dust. The baby will be more comfortable there."

"Then we could use the motor home as an office," Marcus said.

"And you can park it on the slab that my dad used for his boat." Carol pinned Nate with a stare. "It's yours for as long as you need it."

Nate's gaze traveled the room, pausing on Tank, Dalton, Marcus, and then his wife. "Then it's settled. We're going to Eden Rock."

Clay had to speak up. "All of you? Who's going to stay here?"

"I have a few new staff members who will welcome the responsibility. Three recently mustered out and have already volunteered to man the fort for Christmas." Nate turned to Marcus. "We'll leave Reed in charge."

Kay Wolfe leaned around her husband and looked directly at Carol. "Are you sure you want this many people on your property at one time. After all, we're strangers."

"My sister is two years older than I am and would take me to task if you didn't accept my offer. Besides, the ranch is at least twenty minutes from the nearest motel and Clay's clinic. If you set up home base at the clinic, we could be dead before you could get to us."

"Nobody dies on our watch," Nate said. "Let the sheriff know you've hired us. Tell him we're not there to cause him grief, but we will be trying to find out who is responsible for the poison and the fire. We'll square up a couple of things here and be on our way."

****

Carol had been quiet for most of the drive back to Eden Rock. She'd slipped on dark sunglasses, making it hard for Clay to tell if she'd dozed off or was simply deep in thought. She shifted in the passenger seat, turning her head his direction.

"Do you want to talk about it?"

"*It* is a lot of different things. One being finances. I went over the ranch books the other morning. We're in good shape, and I've decided to pay Sue Ellen for her part of the ranch. The bill for Nate and his crew could get expensive."

"You let me worry about that."

"No. I didn't come home to find a man to take care of me. I pay my bills with my money."

"I'm here if you need me."

"Thank you. Having your help and support is the only thing holding me together. I have moments where I wish we'd just signed the contract and walked away, but then I think of the damage that bastard does with his drugs, and I know we did the right thing."

Clay dropped the subject. He pulled into the Four Penny and surveyed the grounds as well as he could in the dark. Sue Ellen had left all the outside lights on, which helped him get a good visual on the place. That somebody had gotten close enough to try to kill the horses and then had set fire to the pasture had his nerves on high alert.

Sue Ellen stepped out on the front porch as he parked. She was very much like Carol, yet very different. Both were beautiful women, but years ago, Sue Ellen had planted her roots in the country while Carol couldn't wait to get away from small town life. Now the two women seemed to have reversed themselves. Would she stick around? Could she? Seeing her holding the sleeping baby, swaying and whispering soft words had made him realize how much he wanted her to stay. Most of all, it had to be her choice made with no reservations, or it wouldn't work.

"You go bring Sue Ellen up to date. I'll check on Pete and then head home."

She reached out and caught his arm, leaned over and kissed him. "Thank you. We'd never get through this without you."

He waved at Sue Ellen and waited until both were inside before driving to the barn and satisfying himself that Pete was fine. Had Carol just told him he was the best friend ever? That was the last thing he wanted to be.

The clinic was dark when he parked around back. He unlocked the rear door, entered and walked through the one place where he felt at peace. Milly had left two folders on his desk, and he paused to read them before he walked into the small room where the sick or injured stayed if they couldn't be treated and sent home.

The cage that he'd placed the older dog in was empty. A smiley face had been drawn on yellow sticky note and stuck to the door. Dancer had gone home with Milly.

Clay had worked for her right here in the same building when he'd been a teenager. It was through watching her and the way she treated her patients that he knew his calling was to care for and help heal animals.

His experience in the military had left him suspicious of his fellow man, and the animals had helped him let loose of that distrust. He checked on the two new patients, made a note in their folders, and returned them to his desk.

Unlike the Lost and Found setup that had access to the living quarters from indoors, Clay had to go back outside and climb the stairs to get inside his home. He took the steps two at a time, unlocked the door, and went inside. The quiet washed over him. He welcomed it, needed the time to think.

He showered, grabbed a towel to dry off, and caught a glimpse of himself in the mirror. When had he last shaved? He took care of that before he crawled between the sheets. He turned on the television, propped up on a couple of pillows, and watched the weather. It was the same story he'd heard on the radio. He hit the off button, hoping the only thing the weather brought tomorrow was the wind.

Apparently, he'd let his hormones do his thinking. Why else would he have let his hopes and expectations about Carol go down the same dead end road? She wasn't in the right place to make a decision about their relationship. Her life was in enough upheaval without him pushing too hard.

****

Sue Ellen reminded Carol of their mother more every single day. The news that three houseguests would be there in two days had prompted an entire house scrub down. They had stripped the beds, laundered the linen, remade the beds, dusted, and sterilized everything that a child might touch. Those chores had been completed yesterday. Currently, Sue Ellen stood eyeing the Christmas tree.

"Do you think we should move all the tree ornaments up higher?"

"I don't. The Wolfe's had decorations out too. We'll place a few books on the end tables and move the breakables to the shelves. Kay said Kevin can pull himself up and stand, but as long as he doesn't turn loose, he can't do much harm."

"Fine." Sue Ellen picked up her cleaning tray. "I'll finish the bathroom. Did you get a couple of racks of ribs from the freezer like I asked?"

"Yes, ma'am." Carol curtsied. "I'm sure they're thawed by now. Would you like me to prep them?"

"It's that or the bathroom."

"You have to stop cleaning. They'll be here soon."

If it hadn't been for the circumstances, Carol would have been thrilled to see her sister so excited. She hoped with all her heart that Sue Ellen's move to the city would result in her finding somebody who would make her happy.

After trimming the ribs and rubbing the family's secret formula on all sides, Carol covered them with foil and put them in the refrigerator. Then she bundled up and walked to the barn. Most of the horses had put on thick winter coats and were in the south pasture, where the line of trees offered a wind break. Pete, Rosie, and the filly, plus two mares due to foal around the first of the year, were kept in the barn. She checked on them, grabbed a small hatchet, and walked down to the large watering trough in the back pasture. She lifted the blade over her head and dropped it against the thin coat of ice, breaking it up so the horses could get a drink. Her hands were getting numb by the time she hurried back indoors.

"Come stand by the fire." Sue Ellen removed her rubber gloves and stored the cleaning tray under the sink. She wrapped her arm around Carol's shoulder and led her to the living room.

"I wasn't going to stay out very long. My initial plan was to check on the mares."

"Dan was going to put cameras over the birthing stalls so they'd be easy to monitor from inside the house. He just never got around to it." Sue Ellen's reference to her dead husband had wiped the good cheer right off her face.

Carol hugged her. "Once you start your new teaching job, your days will be full all the time."

Sue Ellen nodded. "I think so too. But I'm not convinced leaving you here alone is the right thing to do."

"Bull. I'll keep your part-time men busy. Just call me before you come home because the house may not look like it does right now."

Sue Ellen checked her watch. "The smoker should be about right. The ribs won't be ready until supper tomorrow, but we'll figure out something to feed them tonight." She took the ribs outside and was back in minutes.

The sound of an engine drew them to the front door. A motorhome followed by two four-door pickups eased slowly down the driveway. Carol and Sue Ellen put on their coats and went out to greet them. The driver of the huge RV drove past the house straight to the pad their dad had used for his bass boat. He turned around and backed the vehicle up as if he did it all the time.

The door on the first pickup opened. "That's Kay Wolfe," said Carol. "Let's help her with Kevin." Kay had her back to them, unhooking the child from his car seat when they reached her. "Let me," Carol said.

"Thank you." Kay handed Kevin over and introduced herself. "You must be Sue Ellen. I can't help but believe we're imposing. That you are welcoming strangers and a baby into your home is too kind."

"Nonsense," Sue Ellen said. "It's the least we can do. Y'all go inside and I'll stay here in case the men need something."

Carol pulled Kevin's hat down over his ears and tickled him under the chin. He grinned showing a brand new tooth. "I see something new in your mouth. How many teeth do you have?"

"Two on the top and two on the bottom. The bottom ones have barely broken through." Kay shifted the diaper bag from one shoulder to the other. "I always over pack."

Carol showed Kay their rooms and bath. "Kevin and I are going to inspect the tree. Please, make yourself at home."

She and the little boy checked out all the decorations and then went to look out the window. The horses would be up for feeding time soon and she hoped one or more had arrived early. She glanced out and saw that Sue Ellen was giving the four men a guided tour. The one called Tank and her sister were both talking a mile a minute.

Carol pulled back the curtain and hooked it so they could watch. Soon Dalton and Tank got into one of the trucks and left. Marcus and Nate followed Sue Ellen to the house.

Sue Ellen led them into the kitchen, hanging their coat on the horseshoe rack next to the door. "Come to the living room by the fire."

"Dada," Kevin squealed, holding his arms out.

"I'll take him." Nate slipped his hands under Kevin's arms.

"We're going to love having a baby in the house."

Nate chuckled. "You say that now. Is that electrical plug next to the pad where I parked the motor home still hot?"

"Yes. Dad used it to charge the boat's batteries. Flip open the metal box, it's not locked. I heard one of your vehicles leave."

"Dalton and Tank have reservations at a motel in town. They'll stop by and visit with the sheriff in the morning. Just as a courtesy to let him know that we're at your ranch."

"He's a good man, and he'll be happy you're here. Too bad your men left before supper." Sue Ellen looked at Marcus. "You're staying?"

"In the motor home," Marcus said. "It's our central command away from home. We have Wi-Fi, a computer to gather information and share any new intel. It just allows us to stay in touch."

"If the heater in that thing doesn't keep you warm, you come inside. I'm betting the baby will sleep in the room with mom and dad, which means we have an empty bedroom," Sue Ellen said.

Marcus smiled. "Diablo will keep me warm."

"Where is he?" Carol asked.

"In the motor home. We left it running, so I'd better get out there and get the electricity plugged in." Marcus stopped at the door. "But thank you. We'll be fine. Really."

"Then if you'll excuse me, I'm going to see about supper. It will be simple tonight. Tomorrow, ribs, potatoes salad, and pinto beans."

"You feed Tank like that and he might never leave." Kay joined them, taking Kevin from his dad. "You'd better help Marcus."

Nate kissed the baby's forehead and went outside.

"I hate to sound ungrateful, but why four men? It's not like we're under siege," Sue Ellen asked.

"But you are," Kay said following Carol and Sue Ellen to the kitchen. "You've had an attack on your animals and on your property? One of the men will be awake and on guard twenty-four-seven for the next few days. In the meantime, they'll be looking for a way to send Carlos Vega to jail or at least running for the hills."

Sue Ellen backed up to a chair and sat. "Now that you put it that way. Well, I'm scared to death."

Carol immediately knelt in front of her sister. She held Sue Ellen's trembling hands in hers. "We're a lot safer now than we were an hour ago. So are the horses."

Sue Ellen pulled on her bottom lip with her teeth for a minute. "Of course, you're right."

Nate opened the back door and stuck his head in. "I've been expecting to see Clay drive up. He'll probably want a turn standing watch."

"I don't know," Carol said, wondering if she'd pushed him away. "I haven't talked to him."

"I'll let him know we're here." Nate closed the door.

"Carol Ann Penny." Sue Ellen got up quickly. She caught Carol's hands and pulled her to her feet, barely preventing her from tumbling backward. "What did you do?"

"Nothing." Carol went to the cabinets, opened a door, and then started removing plates.

"I think I'll try to get Kevin down for his nap." Kay walked down the hall to their room.

"You made her uncomfortable." Carol tried to turn the focus of this discussion toward her sister.

"Why haven't we seen Clay?"

"I think he's serious about me. Maybe even in love."

"That's not news. He's always been in love with you. Why do you think he never married? His coming home set off more hormone rushes than if Elvis had appeared on the square." Sue Ellen set out tea glasses on the countertop. "But he's still single."

"I have a life, one I worked hard to achieve. I have to be sure that I want to do a complete reversal, give up my career, and run a horse..."

"Don't stop now." Sue Ellen slammed the tea jug down on the countertop. "Say it. Horse ranch. See how easy that was? Horse ranch. Is that so demeaning you can't utter the words?"

"Is that what you think? You couldn't be more wrong. I've watched you work until your hands bled and back ached. Yet you never complained, just moved on to the next problem and seemed to love every minute of it."

"I did love every minute, especially when Dan was alive. I just keep expecting to hear him dust his boots off on the steps before coming inside. Or see him walking around the corner in the barn. It's not that I don't love the ranch, I just can't do it anymore."

"I'm sorry. I don't mean to sound selfish. Of course, you love this place."

"You don't?"

"I really do. I just never found a man who measured up to my expectations. Clay has always been who I measured them by. Is it wrong to want to be sure?"

"Of course not. I see how you light up around Clay. You're happy here. Content."

Carol dropped down in a chair. "It's not a matter of me being happy. I'm not sure I can do it. What if I drive the business into the ground? You've always had an inner strength I've never had."

"That's not true. It took a lot of courage to leave, making this the perfect chance to find out if this is the life for you. If you're not happy, we'll sell. Just not to Vega Industries."

"You're the best sister, ever." Carol hugged her.

"I'm not sure you'll have that much time to decide about Clay. He'll eventually give up and move on." Sue Ellen put a bowl of tuna salad on the table. "I'll get Kay if you'll tell Nate and Marcus it's supper time."

Chapter 6

Nate stepped inside the motor home, carrying a plate of food. "If tonight's supper 'wasn't much,' I can't wait to try whatever she consider a big meal. I brought you two tuna salad sandwiches, pasta salad, and sweet tea. Sue Ellen sent you her apologies for not having dessert."

"The smell rolling off that smoker is going to drive me and Diablo crazy." Marcus bit into the sandwich and moaned.

"You and Diablo okay with the first shift?"

"Sure. We'll make a few rounds early enough to know our way around after it gets dark."

"Finish your supper, and I'll go with you on the first one."

Marcus stopped in mid bite. "You forget how it's done and need a refresher course?"

Nate laughed. "Fuck you. I'm going to walk around. Be back in a few."

"We'll be right here." Marcus tore off a piece of crust and shared it with his dog.

Nate closed the door, put his gloves on, and stared out into the dark, wishing he had a few more hours of daylight, but this time of year that wasn't happening. Why was this piece of land so important? Why this one over the other ranches in the area, a few of which were already on the market? Using a feedlot as a cover wasn't a bad idea, but Vega had to have a plan to get the drugs here to the ranch. Smuggling of any kind through these wide open spaces would be like waving a red flag at the DEA guys.

"You didn't get far," Marcus said walking up next to him. "What are you thinking?"

"That we're missing something big."

"Yeah. You don't think Vega will back off when he learns the Penny sisters brought in help, do you?"

Nate shook his head. "He's too convinced that he's untouchable." They started toward the barn.

Diablo ran ahead. He stopped, sniffed, and peed on everything new. The dog was a good barometer when it came to safety. Nate had often marveled at the animal's sixth sense. Diablo would freeze and almost go into pointer mode when he someone new was in the area, yet a simple movement of Marcus's hand and the dog would relax and accept the situation as okay.

Marcus flipped the switch, turning on the outside lights. The sky was clear but didn't have a sliver of moon. The four-wheeler was designed to carry feed or tools and had a small open bed with on seat. He and Marcus took the front and Diablo hopped in the back.

"Where are we going? The headlights on this thing aren't a lot of help."

"This is a show of presence, just in case somebody is watching. The sooner Vega knows we're here the better."

"True." Nate leaned back. "Drive on."

They drove off the property and down the country road that bordered the front of the ranch. Marcus pulled over at an angle, pointing the headlights toward the pasture.

"This is where Carol found the horse down. Somebody bought those hot house tomatoes that are still on the stems. He bought a lot of them too."

Nate pulled his cell out, called Dalton, and asked that after he dropped Tank off in the morning, he hit the larger grocery stores in the area. Surely somebody remembered a purchase that size. Then he called Clay to let him know that a twenty-four-seven watch had been set up.

The hair on the back of Nate's neck stood up as Marcus backed up and turned around. Diablo's head was resting on the back of the seat in a relaxed position next to Marcus's shoulder. Nate breathed easier.

"It's dark as hell on this stretch of the road. It's the perfect place to sneak up and toss tomatoes or start a fire."

"I'll make a few extra trips out here tonight."

"I'll relieve you around midnight," Nate said.

****

Enrique had been just about to start the car and leave when the headlights had come into view. The night was so dark there was no way he could be seen, but it had also kept him from getting a look at the driver. He'd remained hidden until the four-wheeler turned around and then drove out of sight. He headed to town looking forward to a hot meal and a warm bed.

He'd stopped at the Dairy Dream drive through and placed his order when his cell buzzed. "What's up?"

"Side project for you," Ramon said

Enrique didn't like having his work interrupted. "And the sisters?"

"This man is right there in town. Carlos wants his body found and identified. The rest is up to you."

"Text me the man's name and where to find him," Enrique told Ramon about the caravan of men who'd arrived earlier.

"I'll tell Carlos, but this changes nothing."

"I'll take care of the man tonight. It's fucking cold out here, and I'm ready to end this."

"No witnesses," Ramon said.

Enrique ended the call, picked up his supper at the window, took it to his motel, and then ate it in front of the television.

****

Clay drove past the main house straight to the motor home, parked next to it, and then got out. The door opened and he went inside quickly to avoid letting out any more heat than necessary.

Diablo was sitting in the driver's seat. His eyes trained on him. Clay spoke to the dog and he dropped down and relaxed. "Did you do that or was it because he recognized me?" he asked Marcus.

"A little of both. He's really an incredible dog. It's as if he senses my emotions. Chris, my wife, says he can read my mind." Marcus waved to the small table with a padded bench seat. "Nate will be out in a few. He took guard duty early this morning."

"I spoke with him last night. I'm happy to take a turn." Clay took off his coat and stuffed his gloves into the pocket.

Marcus held up a carafe of something that looked like three-day old coffee. "It's strong but hot."

"Sure why not."

Marcus set the coffee on the table and joined Clay. "Nate says you saved his life."

"He exaggerated. I just shoved him out of the way."

"And took the bullet for him." Marcus saluted with his cup.

"I got to come home and he didn't. There are perks to most things." Clay oversimplified to keep the subject light.

A knock on the motorhome door, ending the discussion as Marcus stood. "Nate wouldn't knock." Diablo again stood with his gaze on the unopened door. "It's Carol."

"Good morning," she said. "I'm looking for Clay."

"Come in." Marcus stepped back.

Clay was already moving. "I'm coming. Is something wrong?"

"No. I thought since you were here we could check on the mares. Will you walk to the barn with me?"

"Sure thing." He grabbed his coat, slipping it on as they walked. "How are you holding up?"

"A little jumpy still. I hope they figure out how to put Vega away soon."

Clay almost wrapped his arm around her and pulled her into his warmth like he had the other day. Instead, he stuck his hands in his pockets and walked beside her.

"Any problem with the new filly?"

"None. She's eating like crazy."

They stepped inside the barn out of the wind and Carol turned to face him. "You've been avoiding me."

He studied her for a minute. "That true. You were pretty clear on the way back from Dallas. I figured you could use some space."

"I don't need space, and I'm sorry if I came across cold. I'm just confused. And scared."

Clay felt his heart rip. "You have nothing to apologize for. Nothing. I pushed you. Expected too much."

She walked to him, removed her toboggan and gloves. "I'm sure of a couple of things and I'd like to tell you."

"Go ahead." Clay braced himself.

"I'm sure that I missed you terribly the two days you stayed away. I'm sure I want you in my life. And most of all, I'm sure that if this doesn't work out it will hurt us both." She lifted up on her toes and kissed him.

Clay buried his hands in her hair and held her head as his tongue ravished her mouth. When he stepped back her lips were wet and swollen. He caught her hand in his and walked to the stall housing one of the pregnant mares.

"I'm glad you told me."

Carol undid the latch and stepped in the stall with him. The mare's belly was distended and heavy. He started at her chest, working his way to her stomach. "Give me your hand."

She did as he asked, feeling the movement of the foal. "It doesn't matter how many times you experience this, the wonder is always there."

"For me too," he agreed. "It won't be long now. The foal is shifting into position." They checked the second mare and then Rosie and her baby before starting back to the house.

Sue Ellen burst out of the door with no coat or hat and ran to meet them.

"What's wrong?" Clay asked.

"I just overheard Nate on the phone. Apparently, Rick Henley was found dead in his home this morning. June Waller was with him."

"What?" Carol asked. "Did you know they were seeing each other?"

"No, and it was awful. His throat had been cut." Sue Ellen's eyes were wide as saucers.

"And June?" Carol asked. Her hand gripped Clay's.

"She must have tried to run because she'd been stabbed in the back multiple times."

"Oh God." Carol's hand covered her heart.

"Let's get you out of the cold." Clay caught each woman by the hand and started to the house.

A shot rang out, Sue Ellen screamed and collapsed.

"Get down," Clay shouted. He dove and covered Carol and her sister.

The motor home door banged open. Marcus, carrying a rifle, and the dog came running hard. Nate burst out the back door and joined Marcus. They hovered over them.

"Get the women inside," Nate barked. "We'll cover you."

Clay pulled a sobbing Sue Ellen into his arms, positioned Carol in front of him and ran toward the house. "We're okay," he said, knowing Marcus and Nate would be right behind them.

Kay opened the door and within seconds they were inside. Clay carried a stunned but alive Sue Ellen to the nearest bed and put her down. Her eyes were glazed from fear.

"Her arm's bleeding." Carol ran to the bathroom and came back with a towel, which she applied Sue Ellen's arm. Tears broke and slid down her cheeks.

Marcus and Nate came inside and closed the door. Marcus stood to the side of the window so he could look out while not becoming a target.

"I called the sheriff," Kay said. "He and an ambulance are on the way."

"It burns," Sue Ellen said as tears fell from her eyes too.

"We'll get you to the hospital soon." Carol used her free hand to push her sister's hair off her face.

"A rifle," Clay said. He was failing miserably at controlling the anger boiling through his veins. "If that slug lodged in something and we can find it, the sheriff will need it."

For the second time in less than a week, sirens ripped through the air as the sheriff's cruiser and an ambulance rushed down the drive.

"I'll go." Clay walked from the room with Nate and Marcus following.

Marcus put his rifle on the breakfast counter in plain view and all three men went outside. Clay made introductions before he and Nate led the sheriff to where Sue Ellen had been wounded. Marcus went inside with the EMTs for a minute, but he quickly joined the sheriff and the team.

"We were just about to start looking for the slug."

"I'm sure you're aware that you can't touch it," the sheriff said.

"Yeah," Nate said. "If we find it, we won't dig it out."

"I'm shorthanded as hell, and my two deputies are at the scene of the first murders this town has had in years. I did take the time to check out you and your team after Dalton and Tank stopped by the other day. If Dalton is willing to be temporarily deputized, he could extract the slug. That would keep the chain of evidence intact."

Nate quickly texted a message, waited a few minutes, and then said, "Dalton and Tank are already on their way."

"I need to talk with Sue Ellen, but first can one of you tell me what happened?"

"Carol and I were walking from the barn when Sue Ellen ran out to tell us that Rick Henley and June Waller had been murdered. We'd headed back inside when she was hit." Clay turned around and pointed to the same pasture Carol had found the sick horse. "The rifle shot came from that direction."

"The other night Nate and I drove the outside of that pasture. We noticed that property bordering the Penny's is nothing but trees and brush. This time of the year it's pretty barren, but you might find enough to hide behind." Marcus stuffed his hands in his coat pocket. "Let's take this discussion inside."

Clay stopped as the EMTs rolled Sue Ellen out on the gurney. Her face was pale as the sheet they had laid across her. Carol walked next to her, holding her hand.

"I'm riding with her."

An EMT shook his head and opened his mouth to speak.

"You can make an exception this time," the sheriff said.

"I'll be there shortly," Clay said to Carol. Even though she wasn't the one shot, his heart folded at the pain in her eyes.

Nate's hand clamped on his shoulder. "Go. We have this. Believe me, she needs you."

"Thanks." Clay went straight to his truck, jumped in, and headed for the hospital.

Chapter 7

Marcus and Diablo left Nate with the sheriff, Dalton, and Tank. Diablo trotted off after a leaf. The wind picked it up and moved every time he got near as if they were playing a game. Marcus had decided on walking because the dog needed the exercise. He sure seemed to love the weather. He looked up at the sky.

"If we get snowed in or worse yet, have an ice storm at Christmas, we're in for a world of hurt." Diablo tilted his head as if understanding every word Marcus had spoken. "You, she'll forgive."

He pulled the toboggan Carol had loaned him further over his ears. The gloves he'd brought from home were good but weren't enough to hold out this kind of bone chilling cold. Marcus whistled for Diablo and walked inside the barn.

The dog froze. The scruff around his neck lifted. A low growl rolled from his throat. Marcus pulled the rifle off his shoulder, spun in a circle, scanning the area as he went. He motioned for Diablo to come sit beside him. Seeing nothing, he stood and decided to climb up to the loft. He knelt and patted his back. Diablo climbed aboard, and up the ladder they went. They crawled over bales of hay to the double windows, one of which he cracked. He watched the heavily wooded pasture for a long time but hadn't satisfied his curiosity. What scent had the dog picked up on?

"Up," he commanded and they went down the stairs.

Again, Diablo growled. And again, Marcus did a visual and saw nothing. They reached the bottom and he said, "Search."

The dog walked down the aisle, stuck his nose just above the dirt floor, and sniffed a straight line to the back door. Marcus opened it and Diablo was headed into the pasture before Marcus called him off.

"Good boy." He ruffled Diablo's fur.

He took the dog to the motor home, gave him a treat, and let him rest. Marcus went inside where Nate, Dalton, Tank, and the sheriff were gathered around the table.

"Stop by my office and pick up a badge." The sheriff stood.

"Before you go, Diablo picked up a scent in the barn. I don't know how far he'd have gone because I called him back after he headed into the pasture."

"You don't think it was an animal?" the sheriff asked.

Nate stood too. "Diablo pays little attention to animal tracks unless he's instructed to. He will alert on anything that feels odd."

"You think somebody has been that close to the house?" Tank asked.

"I don't know. He growled twice, and that's really unlike him."

"Are you done here?" Nate asked the sheriff.

"Yeah. Dalton if you'll follow me to town, I'll get you deputized. I have got to work on the murder. The whole town is probably in shock."

Marcus glanced at Nate but they both remained silent until they were alone with Tank. "How did the sheriff not connect the murder to the sale of this ranch?" Marcus looked at Tank. "You and Dalton gave him all the facts, right?"

"Fucking A we did. And Rick Henley's name came up. We suggested that he'd been sent here to secure the deal for the ranch."

Marcus bit back a chuckle. He liked that the new team member has guts enough to take on anybody that questioned his ability. "Sorry. I wasn't insinuating anything."

"I know that." Tank shrugged shoulders the size of a linebacker wearing his pads. "That sheriff listened to every other word."

"Let's look for that bullet slug, but first see if Diablo will tell us his secrets." Nate pulled his coat off the back of the chair and put it on. "We'd better figure this out if we're going to be home for Christmas."

"Where's Kay?" Marcus asked.

"Putting Kevin down for his nap. She's offered to take over kitchen duties for a while."

Tank shook his head. "Maybe I'll find me a sweet woman like her and settle down."

"Don't let her fool you. She can kick your ass and mine if she sets her mind to it."

"I'll remember that," Tank said, cramming his hands into his gloves. He socked his hat down hard. "Outside."

Marcus and Nate both laughed at Tank's use of a phrase most commonly used by rodeo competitors when they were ready for the gate man to turn him and the bull out into the arena. No doubt he was referring to the ride they were about to take with the weather.

Marcus went to the motor home and opened the door. "You ready to show us what got your hackles up?"

****

Clay stepped behind the curtain in the emergency room only after the nurse gave him the go-ahead. She'd also told him that Sue Ellen had nothing more than a bandage on her arm. She was in shock and upset so the doctor had decided to keep her under observation overnight.

He slapped a grin on his face as he entered. "There they are. I asked that woman at the front desk where the two most beautiful women in the hospital were hiding and she pointed me in here." He stopped at the foot of the bed and patted Sue Ellen's ankle. "It's a dumb question, but how are you?"

"Drowsy. They gave me good drugs."

"She'll be up and ready for her new job in no time," Carol said.

Sue Ellen shifted on the bed and grimaced. "I hated to hear about June. I promised her to keep it confidential, but now that she's gone, it doesn't matter. She was the one who warned me that Vega Industries planned to turn the ranch into a feed lot. She just smiled when I asked her who told her."

"It makes sense," Clay said. "Henley was killed for leaking the truth. June was probably collateral damage."

"You protected us with your body. Could have been shot," Carol said. "Thank you."

"It was reflex. A man protects what he cares for."

Carol stood, released her sister's hand, and walked to him. "I'm glad you're here."

Her eyes were filled with warmth, so he wrapped his arms around her waist. "I'm where I'm supposed to be."

Carol leaned her head back. "This experience has helped me make a decision. The Four Penny Ranch will never be sold. I'm home to stay."

"Hallelujah," Sue Ellen said. "Now get out of here. They're taking me to a room so I can rest. I can't do that with you two in the room."

"Come on. I'll take you home." Clay slipped his hand around Carol's waist and together they walked to his pickup.

"Do you believe we'll ever find out who's responsible for all this? I mean really. To be so evil you'd kill or destroy lives to get what you want, he's probably sneaky enough not to get caught."

"If the bastard can be ferreted out, Nate and his team will do it."

"I hope you're right." She sounded so defeated that Clay pulled off the highway and parked on the shoulder.

"There's a lot going on right now and you're under a lot of stress. I want you to know that your decision to stay made me a happy man."

"Oh, really." Her teasing tone begged for the truth. "Why is that?"

"Because I love you." There. He'd said it. "I was beginning to doubt it before you came home, but you've removed any questions I might have had. I need you more than I need to breathe, but only under certain conditions."

"What are these conditions?"

"That you make your choices with a cool head, and I have to admit that I doubt you can do that now."

"You're wrong." Her tone was serious and warm. "I love you, and that's a fact. So it didn't take us weeks or months to reconnect. I knew it when I walked into the barn and saw you with Rosie. We'll give this town something to talk about."

Clay put the car in park and turned to her. "What did you say?"

"We'll give this town—"

He mentally damned that console between them. "Not that. You said you love me."

"I did?" She bit down on her bottom lip.

Clay was instantly hard. "You did." He could stop looking at her lip.

"And what do you think about that?"

"I love you too."

"Thank God that's settled." She blew out an exaggerated breath.

"Not quite." He dropped the truck into drive and turned around.

"Where are we going?"

"My place. Your house is too crowded and I'm not making love to you in the barn. At least not the first time."

"With me. You'll make love with me," she corrected him.

"I like that even better."

He slid into his parking spot, opened her door, and kissed her even before she'd unbuckled her seatbelt. They stumbled and fumbled their way up the stairs. Once inside Clay turned around and lifted her so she was straddling him.

"Bedroom," she whispered.

"On our way." He hurried across the small space hoping she wouldn't notice that he was a lousy housekeeper. He tossed the bed covers to the floor with one hand and slid her body down his until her feet were on the floor. "I've waited a long time for this, so don't hurry me."

****

Carol felt the heat in his dark eyes. "I'm here for the long haul. Take your time."

"I intend to." His words were almost a growl as he captured her mouth and swept his tongue inside. His kiss was hot, demanding, and sensual, sending that heat to her lower belly. His hands caught the hem of her blouse and pulled it over her head.

She groaned when he placed feathery kisses across her neck down to her bra. Her nipples, anticipating his touch, were swollen and needy. He pulled a rigid tip into his mouth and nipped her through the material.

"Clothes off," she managed to say.

Clay backed up and smiled at her. "As you wish."

Carol sat on the bed to slip off the boots she'd borrowed, but Clay reached down and tugged each one off. Then he toed his off, kicking them out of the way. She stopped undressing and watched as he jerked his pullover off and tossed it toward the boots. His muscular chest had a sprinkling of dark hair on it that ran down over defined abs and disappeared... She lost her train of thought as his jeans and underwear came off in one motion.

"You're beautiful."

"You, babies, puppies and newborn foals are beautiful." He gently pushed her back, unbuttoned her jeans, unzipped them, and then tugged them off. "But I am not beautiful."

He leaned down and kissed her between her breasts, running his tongue across the edge of her bra as he reached around and unhooked it. Almost as if holding a china cup, he held her in his hands, kissing and nibbling on one side and then the other. She was ready to beg for more when he lifted his head and grinned.

"Remember, I'm in no rush." He slid her panties off and joined her on the bed.

His erection pressed into her thigh as he renewed his attention on her breasts. She explored the firm muscles in his back, the slope down to his waist, and the best butt a man had ever had.

He settled himself between her knees and unhurriedly, tantalizingly, kissed her eyes, her cheek, and then neck. He continued his trip down her body, touching and kissing, driving her need to its highest peak.

"This is so much better in real life than in my dreams," he murmured against her stomach.

"You dreamed about me."

"I did. More than once."

He'd driven her to desperation. She needed him. Needed a release that only Clay could give her. His hand slipped down between her thighs, and she lifted her hips in a silent offer. Slowly he inserted a finger.

"Please," she whispered. She opened her legs wider, wanting more. Her fingers dug into his flesh, pulling him closer. "Please," she groaned louder, ready to beg for release.

"But there's a lot more I wanted to do." He smiled again.

Her heart ripped open. "Later." The sound was a mere whimper.

His hand pushed against her thigh, and she spread her legs, giving him easy access. He rolled away and covered himself before returning to her.

"What took you so long?" She smiled as he rose above her.

"If you must know, my hands were shaking a little."

"I like that." His dark eyes locked on hers as he slowly slid inside. She wrapped her legs around his hips and savored every second of his entry.

"You're like a furnace." His words made her tighten around him. His hips moved slowly, allowing her to adjust as he picked up the tempo.

"I won't break."

"Good to know." His lips crashed down on hers as he slammed deep inside her body.

Carol matched his rhythm, losing herself as need consumed her body and mind. Lost in hot and blinding passion, she clung to the edge. When his fingers slipped between them and rubbed her most sensitive spot, she exploded.

His motion picked up as he set a blistering pace and then exploded inside her. His head tilted back and his face was taut as he pulsed through his climax.

His body went ridged for as second before he dropped his forehead on hers. His chest rose and fell rapidly. They lay there for a few minutes before he lifted up and smiled down at her.

"That was far better than a dream, wasn't it?"

"Yes it was." He rolled over on his side, and Carol rested her head on his chest. She smiled when he reached over and gently cupped her left breast. "Think we'll be like this forever?"

"Damn right I do." He ran his thumb across her nipple.

"You don't think I should go home?"

"No." He pulled her into his arms. "You're right where you belong."

She snuggled against him. "I've been thinking."

"That could be a good thing or a bad thing."

She smacked his bare chest with the palm of her hand. "When I marry, I might change the name of the ranch." Her eyes glittered as she lifted up and kissed him.

"Are you proposing to me?" He swallowed hard. She had his full attention.

"Well, I have no intention of becoming your mistress."

Was this really happening? Could any problems, which no doubt they'd have, be hashed out later? "Then I accept. I'd like you to consider allowing me to buy Sue Ellen's half of the ranch instead."

"I think that's a brilliant plan." She rolled on top of him.

Chapter 8

Marcus and Diablo walked to the spot where Sue Ellen had fallen. He turned, standing with his back in the direction that the bullet had to have traveled and extended his arm. "We need to search that area."

"Got it." Tank, wearing a cap, gloves, and a sweatshirt walked a straight line away from Marcus.

"Why doesn't he wear a coat?" Marcus asked Nate.

He shrugged. "Maybe his thermostat is broken."

"Very funny."

Marcus and Nate split up. Each took one side of the direct line Tank was walking. Finding a piece of lead buried in anything was going to be difficult, but they stayed at it until Kay stepped out on the porch and called them into the house.

"What's up?" Nate asked.

"Are you crazy?" She planted her hands on her hips. "The weatherman said it's twenty-eight degrees out there."

"That could be good news. It's probably too cold to snow." Tank removed his cap and dragged his hand through hair that had been cut exactly like Gibbs on television.

"Don't believe it," Marcus said. "That's an old wives tale. Nobody can figure out this winter."

Kay poured coffee for them and joined them at the table.

"We've got more to do outside," Tank said.

"You can warm up first," Kay said. "And where's your coat?"

"I hate them."

A loud noise came from down the hall. "Where's Kevin?" Nate asked.

"In his playpen. Carol gave him a small pan and a wooden spoon this morning. After he woke from his nap, he hasn't stopped banging on it."

"Have you heard from the hospital?" Nate hung his coat on the back of his chair, picked up his coffee, and walked to the window facing the barn.

"No. If I don't hear from Carol soon, I'll call the hospital," Kay said, wincing when a new set of bangs rang out from the playpen. "You're going to have sandwiches for lunch. If Carol gets back in time, I'll see if she wants to use the smoked ribs or freeze them for when Sue Ellen comes home."

Marcus set his cup on the counter. "I'm going to check email. Maybe somebody has a lead that will help us." He and Diablo stood.

"I'll check with Dalton." Nate nodded over a fresh set of clanging from the other room. "See how things are going in town."

Tank grabbed his cap. "I'll go with Marcus. We still haven't walked the route that upset Diablo."

Marcus had barely shrugged on his coat when he opened the door to the motorhome and had to remove it. Tank took a seat at the table, and Diablo jumped up onto his favorite perch so he could look out the window.

"This won't take a minute." Marcus logged on and opened the Lost and Found, Inc. business email. "The daily update from home reads like a robot sent it. I'll bet the guys we left at home are bored but happy not to be out in this shitty weather." He opened a new email from one of the Dallas narcotics detectives and read out loud. "Word is out that Vega put a hit on Rick Henley. Henley must have told June Waller in confidence. Apparently, confidential wasn't in her dictionary." Marcus stopped and reread the last part of the email. "This doesn't make sense. Vega has purchased two feed haulers and a couple of flatbed trailers. He's having a suspected chop shop in Plano customize them. Why?"

Tank opened the jar of peanuts sitting on the table and poured himself a handful. Diablo lifted his head, sniffed the air, and then lay back down.

"Diablo can't have nuts of any kind and he knows it," Marcus answered the questioning look on Tank's face.

"What kind of customization do you need on a grain truck?" Diablo lifted his head and stared at Tank. He shook his head at the dog. "Sorry buddy."

"Or a flatbed? Somebody needs to take a look at one of those trucks." Marcus dialed the office.

"Lost and Found. How may we help you?" Reed Ballatori said.

"You sound like you're having fun," Marcus laughed.

"Loads. Tell me you need me in the field."

"I need you or one of the men who is capable of being stealth."

"I'm the definition of stealth."

"Then get somebody to cover for you because you need to sneak into a custom shop in Plano and find out what bells and whistles are being added to certain trucks."

Reed Ballatori had been part of the team for a few months. His time in special ops had left him a little on the bitter side, but damn, he was smart and an important addition to the business. Marcus explained the situation carefully and gave

Reed all the information he needed to make this op work. Reed knew who Carlo Vega was and how dangerous this could be.

"I'll text you some pictures and an overview of what I learn."

"Vega will have guards twenty-four seven, so be careful."

"I'll be in and out without anybody knowing it."

"Good enough." Marcus ended the call. Opened a bag of dog treats and handed one to Tank. "Give him this."

"Here you go." Tank tossed the snack into the air and Diablo deftly snagged it on its way down. It was gone in two chews.

"Okay, you two." Marcus texted Nate and Dalton the information and the assignment he'd given Reed. "Let's take that walk."

The sweatshirt Tank wore offered no protection from the cold, so Marcus pulled a coat from the closet and tossed it to him.

"Really?"

"Wear the damn thing. Freezes my ass just to look at you."

Tank laughed and shrugged on the coat. "Better?"

"Yeah."

Marcus let Diablo wander. They walked to the barn, checked on the horses, and waited until the dog reached the same spot as before. He tilted his head to the side and a low growl rolled from deep in his chest.

Tank opened his mouth but Marcus waved him off. They stayed about ten feet back and let Diablo explore. His nose was down almost touching the dirt floor. Again, he tracked right to the back door. Tank opened it and stepped back. The dog never hesitated. Out into the cold, he went on the hunt. But for what? The logical answer was that somebody Diablo didn't know had been walking in and out of the barn using this route.

Halfway across the pasture, Marcus called his dog to his side. "Good boy." Diablo turned his head to the side again. "What are you hearing?" The answer hit Marcus so hard he laughed out loud.

"What's funny," Tank asked.

"Let's go inside." He ran to the house with Tank and Diablo right beside him.

Nate jumped to his feet at the slam of the door, and Kevin cried from the other room. The one person, who took it all in stride, Kay, shook her head and went to the bedroom to tend to her son.

"I hope you have something important." Nate sunk back own in the chair.

"Diablo heard something underground."

"Don't tell me he senses an earthquake coming."

"No. He kept stopping and tilting his head to the side like something was going on under his feet. I think I figured it out. We're right that we were missing something. Vega is bringing drugs from Mexico to that barn out there. Underground. He's building a new tunnel."

"Son of a bitch." Nate breathed out a loud sigh. "That's why the bastard doesn't want one of the other ranches. He's spent a ton of money expecting the sale to go through. Nobody, that we know of, has built a tunnel that runs underground this far."

"The DEA closed down a tunnel coming out of El Paso just a few months ago," Marcus said.

"And it was probably his." Tank pulled off the coat and handed it to Marcus.

"Absolutely," Nate agreed. "He buys the ranch, throws up a few cattle pens, and then brings the drugs up into the barn. Perfect. They're sheltered and out of sight."

"And I'm betting Reed finds hidden compartments are being built into those customized trucks and trailers Vega is buying. Trucks pulling in and out of the driveway would be a commonplace sight."

The sound of multiple engines interrupted their conversation. Tank pulled back the kitchen curtain. "Clay and Carol just parked behind Dalton. We still haven't found the slug."

"That's okay," Nate said to Tank. "Dalton knows just who to turn this over to. We never get between a drug dealer and the government unless they ask us to help out. It will take one of those poor souls working in that tunnel or reconfiguring those grain haulers to spill his guts. Then the DEA will move up the ladder to Vega himself."

Dalton held the door open while Clay and Carol entered. Marcus noticed that they were holding hands and both sported the look of two people in love.

Nate stood. "We've kind of taken over your home. Join us and tell us how Sue Ellen is doing and then we'll update you."

"She's fine," Carol said. "They are keeping her overnight but we'll bring her home tomorrow. My challenge will be keeping her down."

"We have other news too." Clay glanced at Carol. At her nod, he announced, "We're getting married."

Kay came into the room just in time to hear the news. She hugged them both. Everyone took their turns saying congratulations.

Nate cleared his throat and everyone returned to their seats. "Thanks to Diablo, we think, heavy on the word think, that we know what's going on. Marcus, he's your dog. You tell them."

Marcus repeated his theory and explained that Reed would have information to them by morning.

Dalton smiled, which was a rare sight. He'd been a loner before joining the company and still hadn't opened up about his personal life. If he even had one. "If we gather enough proof, the DEA will launch an investigation. You may find a hole in your barn floor, but the results of discovering an unfinished tunnel could be far reaching."

Marcus liked how the room felt full of life as they all gathered around the table and discussed what could happen. He certainly hoped a tunnel was what had set Diablo's nerves on edge. Kay went after Kevin. It amazed Marcus to watch Nate take the child, set him on his hip, and then continued to control the situation. He didn't look weak. Not at all. He was still in command. Maybe Chris was right and it was time they started a family.

Carol invited Kay to help in the kitchen; soon they were talking about Christmas memories.

Marcus and Diablo got up. "We're going to the motor home. I'll stay on top of our emails. Who knows when one of our sources will share intel?"

"I'll join you shortly," Dalton said.

Marcus opened the door and Diablo ran into the yard, stopped, and looked up at the sky as huge snowflakes fell. A gust of wind blew and the dog did his best to catch them.

"Tank," Marcus said. "Remember how you said it's too cold to snow?"

Tank got up and started toward the door. "Don't tell me."

"Somebody forgot to tell Mother Nature." Marcus zipped his coat and joined his dog.

Chapter 9

Nate had trouble sleeping again. His mind just wouldn't shut down. It was going to be hard for him to walk away and leave a case still open. But Dalton had spoken with a friend in the DEA office only to learn they were very interested, and everything rode on Reed Ballatori and pictures from his covert mission. Nate didn't like sending one of his men in alone but understood that Reed was an expert and liked to work by himself. If he produced proof that the grain haulers were being modified in a way that would facilitate smuggling, Dalton's contact agreed to come assess the situation.

Clay had insisted that whoever came to the ranch must dress casually and Nate had wholeheartedly agreed. Whoever shot Sue Ellen and murdered the two people in town could still be watching the place. People showing up wearing jackets with DEA in big bold letters on the back wouldn't be smart.

Nate dressed quietly so Kay and Kevin could sleep, went to the kitchen, and then started the coffee pot. Noise outside drew his attention, so he pulled back the curtain. Tank had stayed in the motor home with Marcus last night and they were both walking to the barn.

Nate grabbed his coat, eased out the door, and followed their footsteps in the snow. The white powder came up to his ankles, which had to be a record for this part of Texas. The highways were about to become dangerous if it melted and then froze. Getting home would be a challenge, especially in the motor home.

He stepped inside the barn to the sound of country music. Tank was feeding the horses and Marcus was breaking the top layer of ice off the water buckets.

"Good morning," Tank smiled. He walked to a cell propped up on a bale of hay and turned off the music.

"You two are quite a pair. Marcus, you surprise me. Tank was raised on a ranch but finding you out here shocked me."

"Did I hear my name?" Marcus looked around like he was confused. "My eardrums have been blown out, and I can't hear you."

"Very funny." Tank laughed then stuffed his phone in his pocket. "I was trying to cheer Marcus up. He's not in a good mood this morning."

"I couldn't fall sleep until Reed reported in. We were right about the modifications on the grain haulers. Let's finish here and I'll show you the pictures."

"How can I help?"

Tiny pointed at a bale of hay. "Put two beats, sorry, sections in each horse's netting."

"I know what a beat of hay is," Nate grumbled.

"Sorry, boss."

"And don't call me boss."

"Damn." Tank threw both hands in the air. "I'm beginning to believe neither of you are morning people."

"Ya think?" Marcus laughed.

They finished feeding the animals in the barn. Tank tossed a couple of bales of hay on the four-wheeler to take to the rest of the horses in the back pasture.

"I'll do this so you two can go have a cup of coffee, or maybe two." Tank chuckled as he hopped behind the wheel.

Marcus whistled and Diablo came running. Covered in snow, he shook sending the white flakes flying. "Good dog," Marcus said.

They wasted no time getting inside the motor home. The dog hopped up in the driver's seat and watched Tank.

"I forwarded these to Dalton last night and printed them for us. Take a look while I heat up this coffee."

Nate sat in the one easy chair and studied the pictures. The feed haulers and the trailers had Vega Industries painted on them, but the haulers had an extra special touch. "Smart son of a bitch. The ingenuity wasted on breaking the laws always amazes me. The design is brilliant. A false bottom on the underside that closes and looks like a seam."

"Pretty slick. I got a confirmation of receipt from Dalton at four this morning. So he was awake waiting for these too."

"I'd take Reed into combat with me anytime. He's a good asset."

"Yeah," Marcus agreed. "Reed and Tank fit in with the team right away." Marcus handed Nate a mug of coffee.

"I spoke with Chris last night. It's snowing in Dallas too. She's worried we won't make it home for Christmas."

"Let's see what Dalton has to say. The DEA won't invite us in, they'll invite us out."

"Between the grain haulers and the tunnel they'll have the proof they need. Carol and her sister will be safe."

"Think they'll catch the shooter?"

"Hard to say." Nate's cell buzzed. He read the text aloud. "Dalton says his contact is on the way. We need to get Clay out here and make sure that he's on board with us handing the case off to the DEA." Nate quickly dialed Clay's number and brought him up to date.

"He's on the way?" Marcus asked.

"Yes. He said to tell you Diablo is a rock star." Nate stood. "Let's go tell the Kay and Carol."

They were joined by Tank on the way to the house. "Where's Diablo?"

"In the motor home," Marcus answered.

"It's not fair to leave him out there." Tank stopped a kicked the snow off his boots before going inside.

"You're right." Marcus ran back after his dog. "He doesn't know we're going home either."

****

Clay backed up a horse trailer to the front entrance to the barn, moving in far enough so that no one watching could see what was inside. Agent Preston Hardy jumped out of the passenger side door and helped Sue Ellen out of the back seat of the pickup. The two men escorted her to the house, said hello, and then walked back to the barn. Hardy's western boots, jeans, and heavy suede coat hid the fact he'd been sent to discuss the situation with the Lost and Found crew.

Marcus and Diablo casually walked out to join them. Clay made introductions.

"So this is the dog with the nose?" Agent Hardy reached for Diablo but pulled his hand back when the dog's ears flattened.

"It's okay," Marcus said, and Diablo relaxed. "He's not going to bite unless I tell him. Just hold out the back of your hand and let him get your scent.

They chatted briefly about the freak winter, but Clay could tell that Agent Hardy was ready to get down to business. "Can you show Agent Hardy—?"

"Just Preston."

Marcus smiled. "Sure thing." He scratched behind the dog's ears and waved his hand forward.

Apparently, that released Diablo to wander on his own because for a few minutes, he checked out the horses, sniffing his way around. He walked almost to the far stall that currently housed Rosie and her filly and then stopped. His nose dropped and his hackles rose while he walked a straight line to the back exit doors.

"He hears what we can't," Marcus said. "Come," he spoke to the dog.

"I would call this luck except that's a smart dog. The pictures were enough for a search warrant. This morning when the doors opened at the custom shop, my squad leader, and a few associates along with a SWAT team started an extensive search. We'll prove Vega ordered the false bottoms installed. That's enough to pick him up."

"If you can find him," Clay said.

"We know where he is," Agent Hardy said. "Before I get out of here, I need the owner's permission to open a hole into the tunnel. Somebody down there will turn states evidence."

Dalton drove up just as the small group started to the house. He got out, stopped and shaded his eyes against the glaring white of the snow. "Preston Hardy? What are you doing out in the daylight?"

The two men shook hands and then hugged. Clay almost laughed. He could see the wheels in Nate's head turning. He was already sizing up the agent for a new recruit.

"I got tired of pretending to be an asshole." Agent Hardy grinned.

"Pretending?" Dalton smiled. "I'm glad you're on this case. I was a little uneasy about going home but now I'm okay." He glanced at Clay. "It's a good thing Sue Ellen is moving away, and Carol is marrying you because the ladies love this guy."

"He's already met Sue Ellen. I picked her up before I met up with Preston."

Marcus had had enough of the cold. "Let's take this inside. If you're here to tell us to back off, we'd like some details."

Preston waved his arm toward the house. "Lead on."

Inside, Clay leaned against the counter with Carol next to him and listened to Agent Hardy. The pictures the Lost and Found team had set a ball rolling that seemed to be picking up speed. The assurance that the government would repair any damage done by digging down to the tunnel helped Carol and Sue Ellen both relax.

"We still don't know who shot Sue Ellen. The sheriff hasn't found one scrap of evidence to help."

"That will be one of our priorities. We learned from an undercover agent that Vega hired a new man. We don't have his name but he's from Colombia."

Marcus reached down and stroked Diablo's head. "We have a partner in Bogota. If you get a name for us, we'll track him down."

The coil inside Clay's chest relaxed a little. "As long as the bastard stays on your radar, I'm good."

"We won't forget him," Nate said, exchanging an odd glance with Marcus. "Then at daylight tomorrow morning, we'll start home."

"The roads are horrible," Clay said. "It will be slow going."

"My wife wants us home for Christmas. She and Kay have a reunion planned."

Kay shifted Kevin on her lap. "We have two days to get there. Two of our men and their wives won't be with us, but we'll drink a toast to them."

Clay squeezed Carol's hand. "You're all invited to the wedding."

Tank stood and shook Clay's hand. "When's the big day?"

Carol looked at Sue Ellen. "Spring break, when my Maid of Honor has a few days off work."

Chapter 10

Nate stepped out of the shower, stretched his arms over his head, and then dried off. Damn, he was happy to be in his own home. He slipped on a pair of jeans, a shirt, and tennis shoes before trotting down the stairs to his office area. He stood in silence and stared out the window at the foot of snow covering the parking lot.

The trip north on the frozen interstate had taken hours longer it would have normally, but they'd stopped and helped a few travelers who'd been in too big of a hurry and had paid the price.

Most of Wolfe's Pack were safely tucked away somewhere on the compound. Marcus and Chris had been given the spare bedroom while Dalton, Tank, and Reed were in the barracks, as they called them. Six other members had been dispatched to their home, leaving just the small core group intact.

He went back up the stairs to their living quarters. The smells of Christmas grew stronger with every step. Pies of every flavor had been lined up on the breakfast counter. Ham and sweet potatoes had been bought and prepared along with various other dishes.

The tree was laden with decorations and the floor covered with gifts. Kay had placed and lit candles throughout the house making the entire place smell like evergreen trees. All this fuss would have been too much for him, but it made Kay happy. And as far as Nate was concerned, nothing else mattered.

Voices from behind him drew his attention as Dalton, Reed and Tank pushed, shoved, and laughed their way to the top. It was good to see them so relaxed.

"We're starving," Tank said.

"Then you're just in time," Kay called from the kitchen. "Chris and I have a surprise."

Nate glanced around the room and saw nothing surprising. Chris had poured some sort of red punch into glasses that she and Kay passed out.

"To the dining room please." Kay ushered them into the next room.

Propped up on the table in amongst all the food and dishes were two iPads. Nate's jaw dropped when he saw the faces.

"Merry Christmas from Bogota," shouted Ty and Ana. Their faces filled the first one. Both held up a glass of the same red stuff Chris had handed out.

"Merry Christmas from Murdock," shouted Jake and Holly. Again, they toasted with a glass of red punch.

"I'll be damned. It's the first time Nate Wolfe has been struck dumb," Marcus said.

"Did you know?" Nate asked Marcus.

"I didn't have a clue."

Kay slipped her arm around Nate. "Merry Christmas. It's the closest thing we could get to being together for a reunion."

He pulled his wife into his arms. "Thank you. It's good to see all these smiling faces."

Dalton lifted his glass. "To one helluva holiday."

Also By Jerrie Alexander

Romantic Suspense

The Green-Eyed Doll

The Last Execution

Hell or High Water

Cold Day in Hell

No Chance in Hell

No Greater Hell

A Helluva Holiday

Till Justice is Served

Till the Dead Speak

Someone To Watch Over Me

Flirting With Fate

Skyway to Hell – coming soon

Contemporary Erotic Romance

Come Hard

Come Hot

Come Together

Come Undone

Meet Jerrie

A career in logistics offered me the opportunity to travel to many beautiful locations in America, and I revisit them in her romantic suspense novels.

I write romantic suspense and contemporary erotic romance with alpha males and kick-ass women who weave their way through life's obstacles to emerge stronger because of, and on occasion in spite of, their love for each other. I like to put my characters in difficult positions, make them suffer, and if they're strong enough, they live happily ever after.

My books are written as standalone with no cliffhangers.